TURBO AND PABLO DETECTIVE STORIES

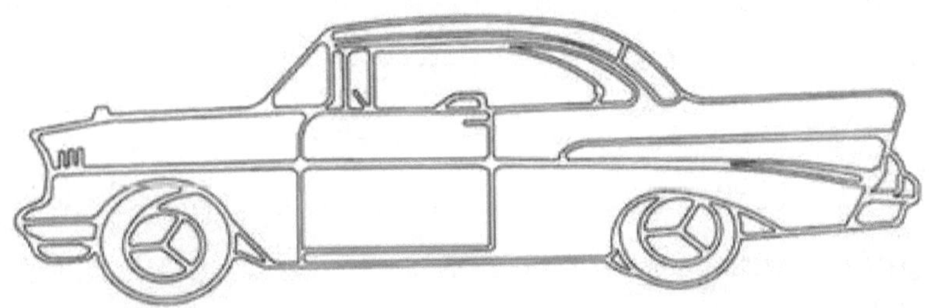

From East Los Angeles

During the 1980's

A Book of Fiction by Robert Nerbovig

Cover Art by Robert Nerbovig

solartoys@yahoo.com

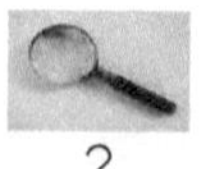

Prologue

East Los Angeles, 1980s—an urban jungle where the sun scorched the pavement by day and neon lights bathed the streets in a garish glow by night. It was a city of contrasts, where dreams and despair coexisted in a delicate, often treacherous balance. In this chaotic tapestry, two figures stood out, carving their path amidst the turmoil: Turbo and Pablo, small-time private investigators with a penchant for justice and a flair for the dramatic.

Turbo, the silent sentinel, moved through the world with an air of stoic determination. His pride and joy was a meticulously restored 1957 Chevy, a gleaming relic of a bygone era. The car, much like Turbo himself, was solid, reliable, and a beacon of integrity in a world rife with corruption. Turbo's eyes, always shielded by dark aviators, missed

nothing. He was a man of few words, but his actions spoke volumes.

Pablo, the former active-duty Marine, in stark contrast, was the voice of the duo—a quick-witted charmer with a knack for reading people and a silver tongue that could talk its way out of almost any situation. Where Turbo provided the muscle and the methodical approach, Pablo brought intuition and a deep understanding of the human psyche. Together, they formed a formidable team, their contrasting styles blending into a seamless partnership that few could rival.

Their office, a cramped space above a bakery on Whittier Blvd., was cluttered with case files, old newspapers, and the lingering scent of pan dulce. The sign on the door, though faded and chipped, still read "Turbo & Pablo: Private Investigators"—a name that had become

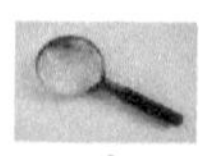

synonymous with hope for the downtrodden and desperate.

In a city where the line between right and wrong was often blurred, Turbo and Pablo became the unyielding sentinels of justice. They took on the cases others wouldn't touch, delving into the dark heart of East LA to rescue the lost, the forgotten, and the betrayed. Their reputation grew with each solved case, their bond strengthening with each danger faced.

Theirs was not an easy path. Every day brought new challenges, new adversaries, and new mysteries. Yet, Turbo and Pablo faced it all with unwavering resolve, driven by a shared belief in the possibility of redemption and the pursuit of truth. In the gritty streets of East Los Angeles, amidst the smoky haze of crime and corruption, they stood as

beacons of hope, ready to fight for those who could not fight for themselves.

This is their story—a tale of courage, loyalty, and the relentless quest for justice in a world that often seemed devoid of it. It is the story of Turbo and Pablo, the guardians of East LA.

Cecelia's Missing Mechanic

East Los Angeles, 1984. The summer sun had just begun its descent, casting long shadows over the city streets. Turbo and Pablo were wrapping up another day of investigative work. The office was cluttered but familiar, with papers strewn about, and a coffee pot that never seemed to be full.

Turbo sat behind his desk, methodically organizing files. He was a man of precision, each movement deliberate, his thoughts hidden behind a pair of dark aviators. Across from him, Pablo leaned back in his chair, feet propped up on his desk, flipping through a worn-out notebook filled with contacts and leads. The quiet was broken by a soft knock on the door. Pablo straightened up, glancing at Turbo, who gave a barely perceptible nod. "Come in," Pablo called out.

The door creaked open to reveal a woman
in her mid-thirties, her face etched with
worry. She clutched a photograph in one
hand and a crumpled note in the other.
"Are you Turbo and Pablo?" she asked, her
voice tinged with desperation.
"We are," Turbo replied, standing up.
"How can we help you?"
The woman stepped inside, closing the
door behind her. "My name is Cecelia,"
she began, her voice shaking slightly.
"My husband, Anthony, has gone missing.
He's a mechanic, and he hasn't come home
for three days. The police aren't doing
anything."
Pablo motioned for her to sit. "Tell us
everything you know, Cecelia," he said
gently.
Cecelia handed them the photograph,
showing a man in his early forties,
smiling broadly in front of a garage.
"This is Anthony," she said. "He left for

work three days ago and never came back.
I found this note in our mailbox the next
day." She handed the note to Turbo, who
read it silently before passing it to
Pablo.

The note was short and ominous: "Stay out
of it, or you'll regret it."

Pablo frowned, his mind already racing.
"Do you have any idea who might want to
harm your husband?"

Cecelia shook her head. "Anthony is a
good man. He doesn't have enemies, at
least none that I know of. But he did
mention something strange a few weeks
ago. He said he saw something he
shouldn't have at the garage where he
works."

Turbo and Pablo exchanged a glance. This
was their kind of case—murky, dangerous,
and right up their alley. "We'll find
him," Turbo said with a confidence that
seemed to steady Cecelia's nerves.

As they gathered more details from Cecelia, Turbo couldn't help but think about the dangerous undercurrents of their city. East LA was a place where secrets festered and danger lurked in every shadow. But it was also a place where people like Turbo and Pablo thrived—those willing to dig deep and fight for the truth.

They decided to start at Anthony's workplace, a small garage on Garfield Blvd. Turbo's Chevy roared to life, its powerful engine a comforting sound to both men. The drive was quiet, each man lost in his thoughts, their minds already working through the potential leads and dangers ahead.

The garage was a modest building, its sign faded and windows dirty. They parked a block away, choosing to approach on foot. Turbo's instincts told him to be cautious, and Pablo's gut feeling agreed.

Inside, the garage was dimly lit, the smell of oil and grease hanging heavy in the air. They were met by a burly man in a stained coverall, who eyed them suspiciously. "Can I help you?" he asked his tone less than welcoming.

"We're looking for Anthony," Turbo said, his voice steady. "We heard he hasn't been around for a few days."

The man's eyes narrowed. "Anthony? Yeah, he hasn't shown up. Probably just ran off. Happens all the time around here."

Pablo stepped forward, his charm on full display. "We just want to make sure he's okay. Any idea where he might have gone?"

The man shrugged. "No clue. Now if you don't mind, I've got work to do."

They left the garage, and their suspicions only heightened. Something was off, and they knew they were onto something bigger than a simple missing person case.

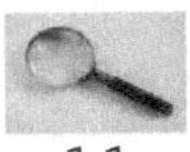

Back in the Chevy, Turbo turned to Pablo. "We need to find out what Anthony saw. Let's start with the people around him." Pablo nodded, already dialing a number in his notebook. "I know a guy who might be able to help."

As they drove off into the night, the city seemed to close in around them. Turbo and Pablo were stepping into the unknown, but they were ready. In East Los Angeles, where danger was a constant companion, they knew one thing for sure: they wouldn't stop until they found Anthony and uncovered the truth.

The case of the missing mechanic had just begun, and Turbo and Pablo were prepared to face whatever lay ahead, driven by their unyielding commitment to justice and each other.

Pablo's contact, Manny, was an old friend from their school days who had since become a bartender at one of East LA's

seedier establishments. Manny had his ear to the ground and knew the whispers that traveled through the city's underworld. If anyone had information on Anthony or his disappearance, it would be him.

They met Manny at Club Intimo, a dive bar tucked away in a forgotten corner of the city. The bar was dimly lit, filled with smoke and the low murmur of conversations. Manny, a wiry man with a quick smile and quicker hands, greeted them warmly.

"Turbo, Pablo, long time no see," Manny said, shaking their hands. "What brings you to my humble abode?"

Pablo leaned against the bar his demeanor casual but his eyes sharp. "We're looking for information, Manny. A mechanic named Anthony has gone missing, and we think he saw something he shouldn't have."

Manny's smile faded slightly, replaced by a look of concern. "Anthony, huh? I heard

some rumblings about a mechanic sticking his nose where it didn't belong. Word is, he saw something at the garage—something big."

Turbo, ever the observer, noticed Manny's hesitation. "What did he see, Manny? And who's behind it?"

Manny glanced around, lowering his voice. "There's been talk about a stolen car ring operating out of that garage. They're stripping down high-end cars, selling the parts, and making a fortune. Anthony must have stumbled onto their operation."

Pablo nodded, his mind racing. "Any idea who's running the show?"

Manny shrugged. "There's a guy they call El Gato. He's been running things from the shadows, keeping a low profile but making big moves. If Anthony saw something, he's in serious trouble."

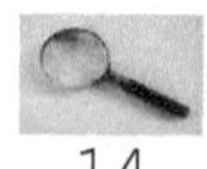

Turbo and Pablo exchanged a glance. They had heard of El Gato, a ghostly figure in the criminal world with a reputation for ruthlessness. This was no ordinary case.

"Thanks, Manny," Turbo said, slipping him a few bills. "Keep your ears open, and let us know if you hear anything else."

As they left the bar, Turbo's mind was already formulating a plan. "We need to find out more about this car ring and El Gato. If Anthony is still alive, he's in deep."

Pablo nodded, pulling out his notebook. "I've got a few contacts we can check in with. Let's see if we can shake the tree a bit."

Their next stop was a chop shop on the outskirts of East LA, known for dealing in stolen car parts. Turbo and Pablo approached cautiously, aware that this was enemy territory. The shop was bustling, with mechanics working on

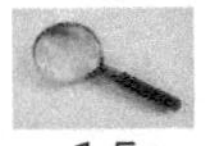

various vehicles, some of which looked suspiciously high-end for a place like this.

A tall, wiry man with tattoos covering his arms stepped forward, blocking their path. "What do you want?" he growled.

"We're looking for information," Pablo said smoothly. "Heard there's been some high-end cars coming through here. We're interested in making a deal."

The man eyed them suspiciously but didn't move. "We don't deal with strangers."

Turbo stepped forward, his presence intimidating. "We're not strangers, and we're not here to cause trouble. We just want to talk."

The man hesitated, then jerked his head toward a door at the back. "Boss is inside. You can talk to him."

Inside, they found a makeshift office where a man sat behind a cluttered desk, smoking a cigar. He looked up as they

entered, his eyes narrowing. "What do you want?"

"We're looking for information about a mechanic named Anthony," Turbo said. "He went missing, and we think it's tied to your operation."

The man leaned back, blowing a smoke ring. "Anthony? Yeah, I know him. Heard he was sticking his nose where it didn't belong."

Pablo's tone turned icy. "And what about El Gato? Where does he fit into all this?"

The man's expression darkened. "You don't want to mess with El Gato. He's dangerous, and if Anthony is mixed up with him, your friend's as good as dead."

Turbo's jaw tightened. "We're not leaving without answers. Where is Anthony?"

The man sneered. "Even if I knew, I wouldn't tell you. But I'll give you a

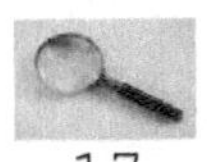

piece of advice—back off while you still can."

Turbo and Pablo left the shop, their minds set on their next move. This case was getting more dangerous by the minute, but they were in too deep to back out now.

"We need to find El Gato's base of operations," Turbo said, his voice resolute. "That's where we'll find Anthony."

Pablo nodded, determination etched on his face. "Let's check with some of our other contacts. Someone's bound to know where he's hiding."

Their next lead took them to an underground gambling den, where they met with a low-level informant named Jimmy. Jimmy, a nervous man with a knack for survival, was always willing to trade information for a bit of cash.

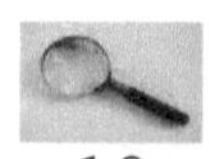

"El Gato's got a warehouse down by the docks," Jimmy whispered, glancing around to make sure no one was listening. "He's been laying low, but that's where he runs his operations. You didn't hear it from me."

Turbo and Pablo thanked Jimmy and headed for the docks, the moon casting eerie shadows on the water. They approached the warehouse cautiously, aware that they were walking into the lion's den.

Inside, they found a labyrinth of crates and machinery, the air thick with the smell of oil and metal. As they moved deeper into the warehouse, they heard voices—angry, panicked voices.

Rounding a corner, they saw Anthony tied to a chair, surrounded by thugs. El Gato stood nearby a menacing figure cloaked in darkness.

"This ends now," Turbo muttered to Pablo, both men steeling themselves for the confrontation.

With a burst of adrenaline, they charged forward, catching the thugs off guard. A fierce fight ensued, fists flying and bodies crashing into crates. Turbo and Pablo fought with everything they had their determination unwavering.

Finally, they subdued the thugs and freed Anthony, who was weak but grateful. El Gato, realizing he was outmatched, slipped into the shadows, disappearing into the night.

As they helped Anthony to his feet, Turbo and Pablo knew their work was far from over. El Gato was still out there, and they had just scratched the surface of the corruption plaguing their city.

But for now, they had won a small victory. They had saved a life and sent a message to the underworld: Turbo and

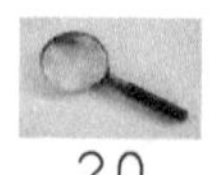

Pablo were here to stay, and they would stop at nothing to bring justice to the streets of East Los Angeles.

A Missing Girl in Boyle Heights

With the glow of the city lights casting long shadows in their office, Turbo and Pablo took a moment to decompress. Cecelia's heartfelt gratitude echoed in their minds, a reminder of why they took on these risky cases. Turbo leaned back in his chair, his eyes drifting to the framed photograph on the wall—a snapshot of the two of them with their first client, a memory of simpler times.

"Think we'll ever get a case that's easy?" Pablo asked, breaking the silence.

Turbo smirked. "Not in this line of work."

Just then, the phone rang, piercing the quiet. Pablo reached for it, answering with his usual charm. "Turbo and Pablo,

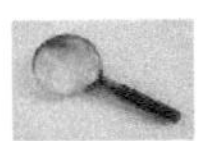

21

how can we help you?" His expression quickly turned serious as he listened. "Alright, we'll be there," he said before hanging up.

"We've got another one," Pablo said, grabbing his jacket. "Teenage girl went missing from Boyle Heights. Her mother's frantic."

Turbo nodded, already moving towards the door. "Let's go."

The streets of East LA were alive with the sounds of the night—sirens, distant music, and the hum of conversations. Turbo's Chevy navigated the city streets with ease, its headlights cutting through the darkness. They arrived at a modest home where a distraught woman awaited them on the porch, her face etched with worry.

Inside, she handed them a diary belonging to her daughter, Isabella, hoping it would provide some clues. As Turbo

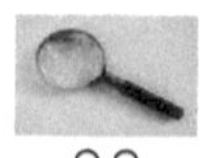

flipped through the pages, he noted the mention of a local nightclub. "El Paraiso," he said, showing Pablo.

The nightclub was infamous for its shady dealings and unsavory clientele. It was the kind of place where trouble brewed, and innocence got lost. They parked a few blocks away, choosing to approach on foot to avoid drawing attention.

Inside, the club was a mixture of flashing lights and loud music. Turbo and Pablo split up, scanning the crowd for any sign of Isabella. Pablo initiated a conversation with the bartender, slipping him a few bills for information. The bartender nodded towards the back room, whispering about a man named Victor who was known for luring young girls.

Turbo and Pablo regrouped, their eyes locking in silent agreement. They pushed through the crowd and into the back room, where Victor was surrounded by a few of his goons. Isabella was there too, looking scared but unharmed.

"Hey, what do you think you're doing?" Victor sneered, but his bravado faltered when Turbo stepped forward, his imposing presence enough to silence any further objections.

"We're taking the girl," Turbo said flatly.

A brawl erupted, the small room filling with the sounds of fists meeting flesh and furniture crashing. Turbo and Pablo fought with practiced precision, years of street experience guiding their every move. They subdued the goons and grabbed Victor, making sure he wouldn't bother anyone again.

Pablo gently took Isabella's hand. "Come on, we're getting you out of here."

They left the club, Turbo keeping a watchful eye on their surroundings. Back at the mother's home, Isabella's tearful

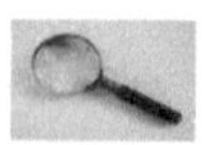

reunion with her mother was another reminder of their impact on people's lives. Turbo and Pablo stood back, giving the family space.

As they drove back to their office, the city seemed a little less dark, the night air filled with a sense of accomplishment. Their work was never easy, but it was always worth it.

"Think we'll ever get tired of this?" Pablo asked, breaking the silence.

Turbo shook his head, a rare smile tugging at his lips. "Not a chance."

In the heart of East Los Angeles, Turbo and Pablo continued their vigil, their restored 1957 Chevy a symbol of resilience and hope. No matter how tough the cases got, they knew they'd face them together, ready to bring justice to those who needed it most.

The Baseball Player is Out

The smog hung heavy over East L.A., the dusty air clinging to Turbo's sweat like a second shirt. Inside their shoebox office, Pablo, his partner, was already hunched over a client.

Pablo, a kid Turbo had taken in a few years ago when he was a scrawny runaway, had blossomed into a sharp PI. His dark eyes flicked over at Turbo's entrance, a silent question in their depths.

"Mrs. Hernandez," Turbo greeted their visitor, a woman's worry etched into every line of her face. "This is my partner, Pablo."

"Thank you for seeing me, Mr. Pablo," Mrs. Hernandez said, her voice trembling slightly. "It's about my Miguel. He hasn't been home in two days."

Miguel, a promising young baseball player, had gone missing after a late-night practice. The official

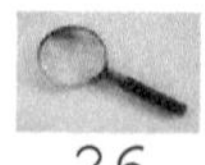

investigation amounted to a shrug and a "runaway" label. Turbo listened patiently, his mind already sifting through possibilities. Disappearances in East L.A. could have a dozen explanations, none of them good.

Attempted Noodle Takeover

Their next visitor was Mr. Chang, a frantic owner of a struggling noodle shop. A competitor had been employing "questionable tactics" to drive away his customers. Turbo, ever the strategist, sent Pablo undercover as a health inspector, a ploy that sent shivers down Pablo's spine but a glint of excitement to his eyes.

The week unfolded in a whirlwind of stakeouts, scouring back alleys for leads, and deciphering cryptic messages left by informants. Turbo, using his old network of contacts, unearthed a

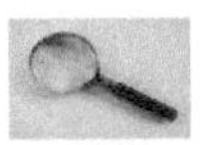

connection between Miguel's disappearance and a local gambling ring preying on young athletes. Meanwhile, Pablo, with his youthful charm and knack for disguises, managed to infiltrate the competitor's shop, uncovering a health code violation so egregious it would make the cockroaches blush.

The climax arrived in a dramatic raid on a dingy warehouse. Pablo, surprisingly adept with a pair of handcuffs he'd procured apprehended the culprits. Miguel, shaken but unharmed, was returned to his tearful mother. Mr. Chang's competitor, facing hefty fines and a tarnished reputation, slunk away, defeated.

Back in the office, amidst the crumpled reports and half-empty coffee mugs, a sense of weary satisfaction settled over them. Turbo reached out and clapped Pablo on the shoulder.

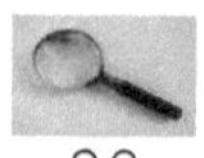

"Good work, kid," he rasped, a hint of pride in his voice. "We make a good team, you and I."

Pablo grinned, a flash of white teeth against his tanned face. "We do, Turbo. We do." He looked out the window at the smog-tinged sunset, a determined glint in his eyes. East L.A. might be a tough place, but with Turbo as his mentor, they were making a difference, one case at a time.

The Screenwriter has Vanished

The following week brought a new client, a glamorous woman named Veronica who oozed Hollywood dreams and desperation. Her husband, a once-prominent screenwriter, had vanished, taking their entire life savings with him. Veronica suspected foul play, a hunch fueled by cryptic phone calls and her husband's recent suspicious behavior.

Turbo, ever the skeptic, took Veronica's story with a grain of salt. Hollywood was a land of make-believe, and Veronica's desperation could easily cloud her judgment. But Pablo, with his youthful idealism, championed Veronica's case. He saw a woman whose world had crumbled and felt a surge of protectiveness.

The investigation plunged them into the glitzy underbelly of Hollywood. Pablo trawled seedy bars frequented by washed-up scriptwriters, their nights filled with the clinking of cheap glasses and whispered rumors. Turbo, relying on his old connections, made calls from his office and managed to pry a name from a bitter ex-producer - a notorious loan shark with a penchant for collecting with his fists.

Meanwhile, Pablo, using his charm and youthful good looks, got close to a young starlet Veronica's husband had been seen

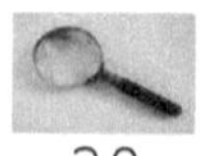

with. The starlet, naive and enamored, revealed a crucial detail - a one-way ticket to Rio booked under Veronica's husband's alias.

The pieces clicked into place. Veronica's husband had staged his disappearance, hoping to frame her and abscond with the money. Armed with this information, Turbo and Pablo raced against time to catch Veronica's husband before he vanished into the jungles of Brazil. A frantic chase through LAX ended with a dramatic confrontation just as Veronica's husband was about to board his plane.

The ensuing struggle, though brief, was intense. Pablo, fueled by righteous anger, managed to overpower the surprised screenwriter and secure him for the arriving authorities.

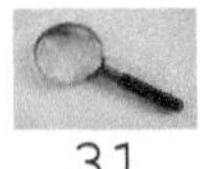

Veronica, tears streaming down her face, rushed to Pablo's side, relief and gratitude etched on her features.

The smog of East L.A. seemed a little less oppressive under the fading California sun, a testament to the unlikely partnership that kept the streets a little bit safer, one case at a time.

My Sister Has Disappeared

The adrenaline from the Veronica case barely faded before another client walked through their office door. This time, it was a nervous young man named Carlos, barely out of his teens. He clutched a worn photograph, his entire being radiating fear.

"Mr. Pablo," Carlos stammered, "it's about my little sister, Rosa. She ran away a few weeks ago, and the police... well, they don't seem to care much."

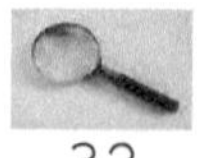

The photo showed a bright-eyed girl with a gap-toothed smile. Something about her innocent face tugged at Turbo's heart. He listened as Carlos, his voice cracking, explained Rosa's recent involvement with a local street gang known as the Vipers.

"They said they'd take care of her," Carlos whispered, his voice thick with shame. "I was scared, Mr. Pablo. I didn't know what to do."

A familiar anger simmered beneath the surface of Turbo's weathered face. These gangs were a blight on the community, preying on vulnerable kids like Rosa. He glanced at Pablo, whose features were hardened with a similar resolve.

Their investigation led them deep into the gang's territory, a labyrinth of graffiti-scarred buildings and wary eyes. Pablo, using his knowledge of the area from his younger days, managed to

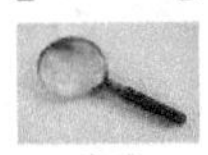

slip into the gang's periphery. He befriended a young lookout named Georgie, promising him a way out of the gang life in exchange for information.

Turbo, using his network of informants on the fringes of the criminal world, unearthed a disturbing truth. The Vipers were more than a petty street gang. They were being used by a ruthless kingpin named El Diablo, who used them to peddle drugs across East L.A. Rosa, according to a disgruntled ex-Viper, was being trained as a courier.

The situation grew more urgent when Georgie revealed Rosa was being prepped for a major drug run out of state. Turbo knew they had to act fast. They devised a daring plan - a two-pronged attack. Pablo, with Georgie's help, would create a diversion within the gang, giving Turbo a window to grab Rosa before she was shipped out.

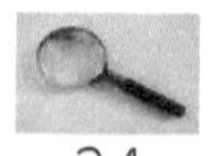

The night of the operation arrived, cloaked in an oppressive darkness. Pablo, a nervous knot tight in his stomach, infiltrated a gang meeting under the pretense of delivering a message. He created a scene, shouting fabricated orders about a rival gang attack. Chaos erupted, drawing the Vipers' attention away.

Turbo, using his knowledge of the gang's hangouts from his clues, raced through the maze of buildings. He finally found Rosa, a scared but determined girl, being bundled into a van. A fierce struggle ensued. One of the gang members, a hulking young man with a shaved head, swung at Turbo. The pain in his leg flared, causing him to stumble. But before the blow landed, a figure appeared beside him.

It was Pablo, having evaded the chaos at the meeting. He used his superior

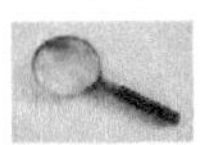

agility to disarm the goon, landing a
well-placed kick that sent him sprawling.
Together, they overpowered the remaining
Viper thugs and rescued Rosa.

The aftermath was a whirlwind of police
reports and witness statements. The
rescued Rosa, tearful but relieved, gave
a statement about El Diablo's operation.
The police, finally spurred to action,
launched a raid on El Diablo's hideout.
Days later, news reports announced the
arrest of El Diablo and the dismantling
of his operation. Carlos, his face
beaming with gratitude, embraced Turbo
and Pablo at their office. Rosa, shy but
hopeful, stood beside him, a bright spot
in the grimy reality of East L.A.

But even as the city celebrated a
victory, the weary detectives knew this
was just one battle in a long war. The
victory came at a cost. Turbo's leg
injury had worsened, the pain a constant

36

reminder of the price of their work. He found himself spending more time at the doctor's office than at stakeouts.

The burden of their investigations began to weigh heavily on Pablo. He loved the rush of adrenaline, and the satisfaction of bringing justice, but the violence and the relentless parade of heartbreak took their toll. One night, as they sat in their dimly lit office, Pablo voiced his doubts.

"Turbo," he said, his voice quiet, "what if this... what if it's too much? I don't know how much more I can handle."

Turbo studied Pablo, seeing the weariness etched on his once-youthful face. He understood. This wasn't just a job; it was an emotional rollercoaster, one that threatened to take its toll on the strongest spirit.

"It's okay, kid," Turbo said, his voice gruff but gentle. "This life ain't for

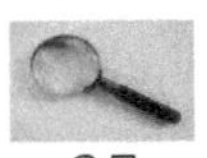

the faint of heart," Turbo finished, his voice gruff but gentle. "But listen close, Pablo. You have a fire in you, a sense of justice that most folks lose somewhere along the way. Don't let it go out. This city needs people like you, even if it ain't always easy."

Pablo stared out the window, the neon glow of East L.A. painting a vibrant yet harsh picture. He saw the flickering hope in the eyes of families they'd helped, the fear etched on the faces of those trapped in a cycle of violence. He knew Turbo was right. This wasn't just a job; it was a calling.

The following weeks were a period of readjustment. Turbo, forced to take a more passive role, spent his days strategizing from his desk, frustration gnawing at him with every throbbing pain in his leg. Pablo, burdened with the sole responsibility of fieldwork, found

himself questioning every move. The camaraderie they shared, the unspoken language of trust and support, seemed strained.

Roberto is Getting a Bum Rap

One rainy afternoon, a new client walked through the door. She was an elderly woman named Mrs. Rodriguez her face etched with worry lines deeper than the canyons that ringed the city. Her grandson, Roberto, a promising young artist, had been arrested for vandalism. But Mrs. Rodriguez was adamant Roberto was innocent.

"He wouldn't do something like that, Mr. Pablo," she pleaded, her voice trembling. "He's a good boy. He was just painting a mural, trying to beautify the neighborhood."

Turbo, intrigued by the case and eager to get Pablo back on track, decided on a

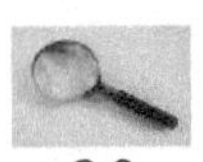

different approach. He sent Pablo undercover, not as a tough investigator, but as a fellow artist seeking inspiration in the neighborhood.

Pablo, with his natural charisma and genuine interest in art, quickly gained the trust of the local youth. He learned about a rival gang, the Dragons, who were notorious for defacing murals created by other artists. Roberto, it turned out, was caught in the crossfire, his vibrant mural mistaken for a Dragon tag.

The investigation took a dangerous turn when Pablo witnessed the Dragons vandalizing a freshly painted mural. He barely managed to escape their notice, the adrenaline rush reminding him of the thrill and the risk that came with their line of work.

Back at the office, Pablo laid out the information. Turbo, his eyes gleaming with a spark of his old fire, formulated

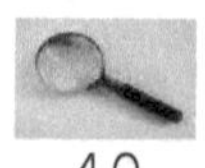

a plan. They would use Roberto's artistic talents to set a trap for the Dragons. With Mrs. Rodriguez's permission, they provided Roberto with art supplies and a new wall to showcase his work. Word spread through the neighborhood, and soon, a vibrant image of a phoenix rising from the ashes began to take shape.

As expected, the Dragons showed up, enraged to see their territory "marked" by another artist. But this time, they were met not by fists, but by a swarm of cameras. Turbo, using his old connections with local news outlets, had tipped them off anonymously.

The news footage, capturing the Dragons vandalizing a beautiful mural in front of a crowd of outraged residents, went viral. Public pressure forced the police to take action, leading to the arrest of the Dragon gang leaders. Roberto, not

only cleared of the charges, became a local hero, his mural a symbol of hope and resilience.

The successful resolution of the case marked a turning point for Turbo and Pablo. They had learned to adapt and to utilize their strengths and weaknesses as a team. Turbo, by accepting his limitations, became a strategist and mentor. Pablo, by embracing the responsibility, honed his skills and developed a sense of confidence.

Miguel's Cold Case Killing

Their next case brought them face to face with a ghost from Turbo's past. A woman named Sylvia walked through the door, her tear-stained cheeks mirroring the rain lashing against the windows. She was the widow of Turbo's former partner, Miguel, the man who had been shot alongside him all those years ago.

"They found Miguel's killer," she said, her voice hoarse. "But the police say it's a cold case. They're not interested in digging any deeper."

Turbo's face hardened. Miguel's death had been a constant weight on his conscience, a reminder of the brutality of their world. He couldn't let Sylvia down. Not again.

The investigation into Miguel's case was a walk down a dark memory lane. They revisited old haunts, talked to ghosts of the past, and unearthed a network of corruption that ran deep within the city's underbelly.

The trail led them to a powerful crime boss known as El Tiburon (The Shark). Miguel, it turned out, had stumbled upon evidence of El Tiburon's involvement in human trafficking. He had been silenced before he could expose the truth.

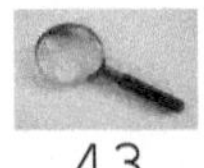

The investigation into Miguel's case became a personal crusade for Turbo. Driven by a potent mix of grief and determination, he pushed himself past his physical limitations, the throbbing pain in his leg a constant companion. Pablo, sensing Turbo's emotional turmoil, doubled his efforts, his youthful spirit tempered with a newfound resolve.

Their investigation led them to a network of informants on the fringes of El Tiburon's operation. These were people who lived in fear, their voices barely whispers in the dark alleys and smoke-filled dives. One of them, a weary bartender named Hector, reluctantly revealed a shipment of El Tiburon's victims was scheduled to leave the city harbor that night.

Turbo, his mind racing, formulated a desperate plan. It was a high-risk operation, one that could expose them

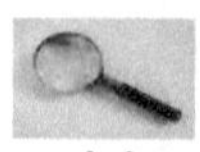

directly to El Tiburon's ruthless
enforcers. He laid out the plan for
Pablo, his voice gravelly with emotion.
"Kid," Turbo rasped, "this is gonna be
rough. You might have to go it alone on
this one."
Pablo met his gaze, his eyes firm. "No
way, Turbo. We face this together.
Always."
That night, under the cloak of a storm-
wracked sky, they infiltrated the
bustling harbor. The air hung heavy with
the smell of diesel fuel and salt spray.
Using their knowledge of the docks
gleaned from informants, they located the
container suspected of holding El
Tiburon's victims.
The lock was a formidable obstacle.
Turbo, gritting his teeth against the
pain, wrestled with a crowbar, his
muscles screaming in protest. Just as he
managed to pry the lock open, a pair of

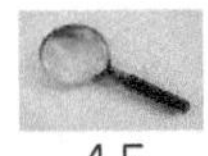

headlights sliced through the darkness. El Tiburon's men.

A desperate chase ensued. Pablo, using his agility, weaved through stacks of containers, drawing the thugs away from Turbo. He led them on a frantic chase through the labyrinthine maze of the dockyard, his heart pounding against his ribs.

Meanwhile, Turbo, his injured leg a dead weight, stumbled towards the open container. Inside, huddled in the darkness, were frightened faces - men, women, and even children. He yelled for them to stay quiet as he fumbled with his phone, sending a pre-arranged signal to the police contact he'd cultivated during the investigation.

Just as the police sirens wailed in the distance, El Tiburon's men caught up to Pablo. A brutal fight ensued. Pablo, fueled by adrenaline and a sense of

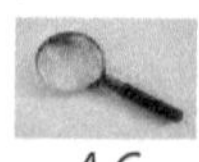

righteous anger, managed to hold his own against the bigger men, his street smarts and training paying off.

The arrival of the police turned the tide. El Tiburon's men scattered like roaches. The rescued victims emerged from the container, blinking in the flashing lights, their faces etched with relief and gratitude.

News of the operation broke the next day. El Tiburon's human trafficking ring was exposed, and a citywide manhunt ensued. The rescue at the harbor, spearheaded by the unlikely duo of a grizzled veteran PI and his sharp young partner, became a symbol of hope in a city often plagued by despair.

The resolution of Miguel's case brought a bittersweet closure for Turbo. He finally laid his guilt to rest, honoring his fallen partner's memory. Standing beside Pablo in their office, a sense of

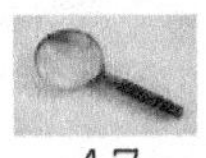

camaraderie and respect hung heavy in the air.

"You did good, kid," Turbo said, a hint of pride in his voice. "Real good."

Pablo nodded, a newfound maturity settling in his eyes. "We did good, Turbo. We did good."

Maria's Missing Brother

The victory, however, was short-lived. The city's underbelly remained a place of shadows and secrets. A new client walked through the door just as they were contemplating their next move. It was a young woman named Maria, her face pale with fear. Her brother, a construction worker, had gone missing from a work site on the outskirts of the city.

"The police say it's an accident," Maria whispered, "but I know something's wrong. He wouldn't just disappear."

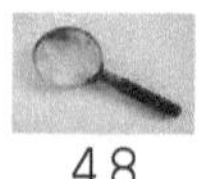

Turbo and Pablo exchanged a glance. The city might be celebrating their recent victory, but their work was far from over. They were the guardians of the forgotten corners of East L.A., and as long as there were those in need, they would continue their fight for justice, one case at a time.

The construction site on the outskirts of the city loomed large and desolate, a skeletal frame of steel and concrete against the fading afternoon sun. Maria, her anxiety a palpable presence, pointed at a spot where her brother, Eddie, had last been seen.

"He was working on that platform," she said, her voice trembling slightly. "They said a high wind knocked him off, but it just doesn't seem right."

Turbo, his cane tapping a steady rhythm against the dusty ground, surveyed the scene. The platform in question seemed

precariously balanced, a frayed rope its only safety line. A pang of suspicion shot through him. This looked more like a staged accident than a tragic mishap. Pablo, ever-observant, noticed a fresh scuff mark on the metal railing near the platform. It was a sign of struggle, a clue that corroborated Maria's suspicion. The official narrative reeked of a cover-up, and Turbo and Pablo were determined to uncover the truth.

Their investigation led them to a maze of permits, shady subcontractors, and a ruthless developer named Mr. Thorne. Thorne, a man with a steely gaze and a reputation for cutting corners, was pushing for an accelerated construction timeline. It seemed all too convenient that Eddie, a vocal critic of the unsafe working conditions, had vanished just as these time constraints intensified.

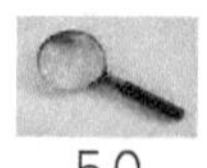

Their only lead came from a gruff construction worker named Hank, a weathered man with a mistrustful glint in his eye. Hank, after a few rounds of beers at a local dive bar, revealed details about a heated argument between Eddie and a Thorne representative just before his disappearance.

Armed with this information, Turbo devised a plan. Pablo, using his youthful appearance and disarming charm, would pose as a potential employee seeking work at the site. His mission was to gain access and gather any evidence that could point towards foul play.

Meanwhile, Turbo would discreetly contact a local building inspector, a man with a grudge against Thorne's unethical practices. Together, they hoped to expose the safety violations and uncover

any potential evidence that could link Thorne to Miguel's disappearance.

Pablo's first day on the job was a baptism by fire. He witnessed firsthand the lax safety measures and the constant pressure to meet unrealistic deadlines. He befriended a young worker named Luis a man disillusioned by the industry's disregard for worker safety. Luis, sensing Pablo's genuineness, agreed to keep an eye out for any suspicious activity.

One night, while the site was supposedly deserted, Pablo discovered a hidden compartment within a construction trailer. Inside, he found a stack of documents – falsified safety reports and a logbook detailing hush money payments to injured workers.

Just as Pablo was about to escape with this incriminating evidence, he was spotted by a security guard. A frantic

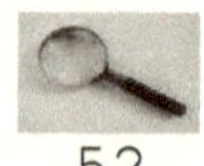

chase ensued, Pablo navigating the maze of scaffolding and steel beams with surprising agility. He managed to evade capture, but the element of surprise was gone.

News of Pablo's near-capture reached Turbo. He knew it was time to put their plan into action. The building inspector, a man named Johnson, arrived at the site with a warrant, citing numerous safety violations. The construction was halted, much to Thorne's fury.

However, Eddie was still missing. The pressure mounted, and Maria's hope began to dwindle. One evening, a desperate phone call arrived from Hank, the gruff construction worker. He claimed to have overheard something incriminating at a local bar frequented by Thorne's associates.

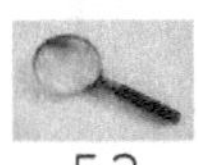

Turbo and Pablo rushed to the bar, a dingy establishment reeking of stale beer and desperation. Hank pointed them towards a group of men huddled in a corner booth. As they approached, they recognized one of the men - Thorne's right-hand man, a hulking thug named Bruno.

Bruno, seeing them, grew tense. A heated argument erupted, accusations flying back and forth. A struggle ensued, the scuffle spilling out onto the street. Turbo used his cane more as a weapon than a support, while Pablo's street smarts came into play as they fought off Bruno and his associates.

The commotion attracted the attention of a passing police patrol car. The officers, alerted of the ongoing investigation at the construction site, apprehended Bruno and his accomplices. Under interrogation, and fearing a more

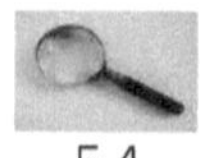

severe punishment, Bruno revealed a horrifying truth.

Eddie, in his attempt to expose the dangerous shortcuts, had stumbled upon evidence of a planned structural sabotage meant to expedite construction. Thorne's men, fearing exposure, had overpowered Eddie and dumped him in a remote quarry. With this information, the police launched a search of the quarry. The next morning, they found Eddie, unconscious but alive, buried beneath a pile of rubble.

The news of Eddie's rescue brought immense relief to Maria, whose tears of gratitude washed away days of worry. The city celebrated the brave construction worker and the tenacious PIs who brought him back. However, for Turbo and Pablo, the victory was bittersweet.

The incident exposed a systemic problem plaguing the construction industry, a web

of greed that prioritized profit over human life. Thorne, facing multiple charges, including attempted murder and bribery, was vilified by the media. But they knew this was just one cog in a larger machine; there would always be another Thorne lurking in the shadows. The following weeks were a whirlwind of court appearances, witness testimonies, and sorting through the aftermath of the case. A sense of fatigue settled over them, both physical and emotional. Turbo, his leg throbbing incessantly, realized his body was pushing its limits. He spent more time at the doctor's than at his desk, the frustration etched on his face.

The Contaminated Building

One day, a familiar face walked into their office. It was Luis, the young construction worker Pablo had befriended

on the Thorne site. He looked hesitant his youthful bravado replaced by a nervous demeanor.

"Mr. Pablo," Luis stammered, "I don't know if this is any good, but I think you guys should see this."

He handed them a worn photograph - a picture of a derelict building in a dilapidated neighborhood. Luis explained how he overheard a conversation at the worksite about demolishing the building, a project riddled with whispers of asbestos contamination and shady deals.

A spark of determination flickered in Pablo's eyes. This was an opportunity to make a difference, to prevent another tragedy before it happened. He turned to Turbo, a question hanging in the air.

"Think we can handle one more case, Turbo?"

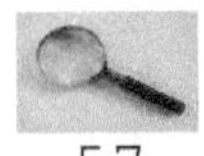

Turbo, despite his fatigue, felt a familiar sense of purpose stir within him. "We can't let them get away with this, kid. Let's do it."

Their investigation into the derelict building led them down a rabbit hole of bureaucratic red tape and conflicting reports. The building, once a vibrant community center, had been abandoned decades ago, its ownership shrouded in a veil of mystery. The demolition contract, awarded to a company with a checkered environmental record, seemed rushed through with minimal public scrutiny.

They needed an ally within the system, someone willing to fight the tide of corruption. Through an old network contact, they met Olivia, a tenacious city councilwoman known for her activism against environmental injustices.

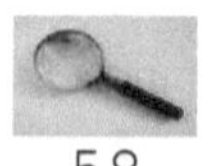

Olivia, after reviewing their findings, felt a sense of urgency.

"This is bigger than just one building," she said, her voice firm. "This could be another Thorne waiting to happen."

Together, they devised a two-pronged strategy. Pablo, using his youthful façade and charm, infiltrated the demolition company, hoping to uncover their plans and any damning evidence. He posed as a recent graduate eager to prove himself, slowly gaining the trust of the foreman, a gruff man with a cynical view of the world.

Meanwhile, Turbo and Olivia, with the help of a team of independent environmental consultants, secured an injunction on the demolition process, citing potential asbestos contamination. The news sent shockwaves through the city council, sparking debates and media scrutiny.

Pablo, undercover at the demolition company, witnessed firsthand their disregard for safety protocols. They planned to demolish the building under the cover of darkness, hoping to avoid any public scrutiny. He managed to sneak a hidden camera into the foreman's office, capturing incriminating footage of them discussing the asbestos issue and their intention to cut corners.

The night of the planned demolition arrived, cloaked in a heavy veil of tension. Turbo, Olivia, and a team of concerned citizens staged a peaceful protest outside the derelict building. Pablo, his heart pounding against his ribs, sent them a live feed from the hidden camera, exposing the demolition company's blatant disregard for safety regulations.

The police, alerted by Olivia's office, arrived on the scene just as the

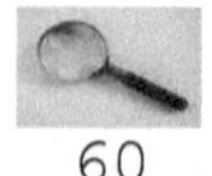

demolition crew prepared to initiate the process. The footage captured by Pablo provided irrefutable evidence, forcing the demolition to be halted. News of the bust exposed the entire operation, with public outrage mounting against the corrupt company and the complicit officials.

The fallout from the case was significant. The demolition company faced a barrage of lawsuits, their reputation tarnished. An investigation into the ownership of the building revealed a tangled web of shell companies and offshore accounts. Olivia heralded as a champion of the community, launched a campaign for a stricter environmental protection policy.

The victory, however, came at a cost. The ordeal had taken a toll on Turbo. His leg injury worsened, the constant pain a gnawing reminder of his

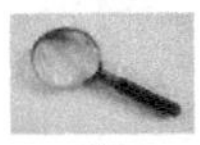

limitations. He confided in Pablo, his
voice laced with a weary resignation.

"Kid," Turbo rasped, his weathered face
etched with a struggle between pride and
pain. "Maybe it's time I called it quits.
I can't keep pushing my body like this.
This case took more out of me than I let
on."

Pablo felt a pang of fear twist in his
gut. Turbo had been more than just a
partner; he was a mentor, a father figure
in a way. The thought of running the
agency alone, facing the gritty
underworld without Turbo by his side, was
daunting.

"Turbo," he said, his voice firm despite
the tremor in his heart, "you built this
place. You taught me everything I know.
But you can't just walk away. What about
all the others who need us? What about
the fight you always talk about?"

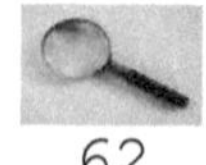

Turbo studied Pablo, his gaze filled with a mixture of amusement and recognition. He saw a reflection of his youthful fire in Pablo's eyes, the same unwavering determination he possessed all those years ago. He knew Pablo was right. Giving up wasn't his style. It wasn't the legacy he wanted to leave behind.

"Alright, kid," Turbo said, a hint of a fighting spirit returning to his voice. "You win. But on one condition."

"Anything," Pablo replied eagerly.

"You become the muscle," Turbo said with a smirk, "and I become the brains. We adapt, just like we always do."

A relieved smile spread across Pablo's face. "Deal," he said, a sense of renewed energy surging through him.

The following weeks were a period of reinvention for their partnership. Turbo remained the strategist, his sharp mind analyzing cases and orchestrating

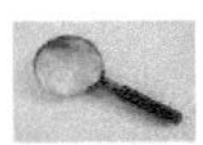

investigations from his desk. Pablo, now the lead investigator, honed his skills in surveillance, hand-to-hand combat, and navigating the treacherous streets with an agility that often left even the most seasoned criminals in awe.

Sofia Is Missing

The following week, a new client walked through their door, a man named Javier Ramirez, his face etched with worry lines deeper than the canyons that ringed the city. His teenage daughter, Sofia, had gone missing, and the police seemed to be treating it as a runaway case.

"She wouldn't just leave," Ramirez pleaded, his voice thick with despair. "There has to be more to it."

Turbo studied the frantic man, a spark of recognition flickering in his memory. Ramirez, it turned out, was a former gang member, a man who'd left that life behind

years ago. A life Turbo knew all too well.

"Did Sofia get mixed up with anything?" Turbo asked, his voice gruff but laced with empathy.

Ramirez hesitated, then admitted Sofia had been volunteering at a local community center, a place known for helping reformed gang members reintegrate into society. He feared a rival gang might be targeting her, using her as leverage to get back at him.

The investigation took them into a world of fragile second chances and the ever-present pull of the past. Pablo, using his knowledge of the street scene, infiltrated the community center, posing as a troubled youth seeking guidance. He befriended a group of teenagers, slowly gaining their trust and piecing together the puzzle.

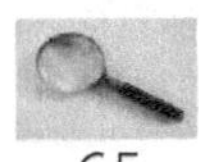

It turned out Sofia had witnessed a drug deal involving a local gang called the Vipers, the very same gang Ramirez had left behind. The Vipers, led by a ruthless young leader named Diablo, were furious and viewed Sofia as a loose end. Turbo, using his old connections on the fringes of the gang world, confirmed their suspicions. He learned Diablo planned to use Sofia as a bargaining chip to force Ramirez back into the gang, a move that would shatter the fragile peace he'd built for himself and his family. The situation demanded a delicate approach. A confrontation with the Vipers could put Sofia in even greater danger. Turbo and Pablo devised a two-pronged strategy. Pablo, using his street smarts, would infiltrate the Vipers' hangout, hoping to locate Sofia and create a diversion. Meanwhile, Turbo would anonymously tip off a police task

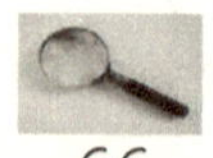

force known for their work in gang rehabilitation, hoping they could intervene before violence erupted.

The operation unfolded under the cloak of a simmering city night. Pablo, his heart pounding against his ribs, snuck into the Vipers' hangout, a graffiti-scarred building reeking of stale drugs and desperation. He spotted Sofia, held captive in a back room. A brutal fight ensued as he tried to free her, drawing the attention of the Vipers and their leader, Diablo.

Just as Diablo was about to unleash his fury on Pablo, a team of police officers from the task force burst through the front doors. They'd been tipped off about the location and the potential hostage situation. A tense standoff ensued, but ultimately, the outnumbered Vipers surrendered.

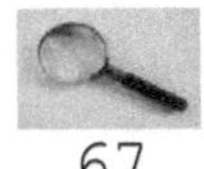

Sofia, shaken but unharmed, was reunited with her tearful father. Ramirez, his eyes filled with gratitude, expressed his heartfelt thanks to Turbo and Pablo. "You saved my daughter," he said, his voice thick with emotion. "And you saved me from becoming who I used to be."
News of the raid resonated through the city. It highlighted the importance of second chances and the need for programs that helped former gang members rebuild their lives. The Vipers, crippled by the arrest of their leader, were forced to lay low.
Back in their office, a sense of quiet satisfaction hung in the air. Turbo, despite the throbbing pain in his leg, felt a sense of accomplishment. They had not only saved a life but also offered a flicker of hope for a city struggling with gang violence.

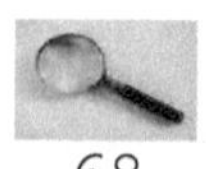

"Another case closed," Pablo said, a hint of pride in his voice.

Turbo nodded, a weary but determined glint in his eyes. "Another one, kid. But you know what? I wouldn't want to do it with anyone else."

Pablo grinned, the camaraderie between them a silent promise. As long as they had each other, they would continue to fight for justice, their unique partnership a beacon of hope in the often-bleak streets of East L.A. The city lights twinkled outside their window, a testament to the resilience of the human spirit and the unwavering determination of two unlikely heroes.

Where is My Daughter

The air hung heavy with the scent of rain-soaked pavement as a haggard woman, Mrs. Rodriguez, shuffled into Turbo & Pablo Investigations. Her eyes, red-

rimmed and weary, reflected the storm brewing outside. In her trembling hands, she held a worn photograph, a faded image of a vibrant young woman with a bright smile.

"This is my granddaughter, Isabella," she rasped, her voice hoarse. "They say she's run away, but I know something's wrong. She wouldn't just leave like this."

Turbo studied the photo of the young woman's smile a stark contrast to the desperation etched on Mrs. Rodriguez's face. A familiar pang of responsibility tugged at his heart. Missing person cases, especially those involving young women, often led to dark corners of the city.

"Tell me about Isabella, Mrs. Rodriguez," Pablo interjected his youthful energy a welcome contrast to Turbo's gruff demeanor.

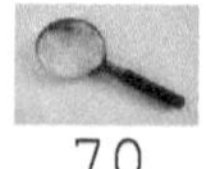

As Mrs. Rodriguez recounted Isabella's story, a chilling truth emerged. Isabella, a gifted artist, had recently begun volunteering at a local women's shelter. There, she befriended a group of women who had escaped human trafficking rings. Isabella, with a fiery spirit and a knack for storytelling, documented their experiences through her art.

Their investigation led them to the shelter, a safe haven for the most vulnerable in the city. The women there, wary at first, slowly warmed up to Pablo's empathetic approach. They confirmed Isabella had become increasingly agitated, haunted by the stories of the women. She had started asking questions, digging deeper into the details of their escape, particularly about a ruthless trafficker known only as "The Wolf."

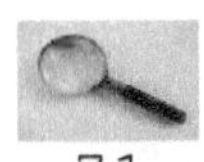

Turbo, using his network of informants, confirmed rumors about The Wolf. He was a ghost, a man who operated with terrifying efficiency, his tentacles reaching deep into the city's underbelly. Isabella's curiosity, it seemed, had inadvertently put her in his crosshairs. Determined to protect the remaining women at the shelter and to find Isabella Pablo and Turbo formulated a risky plan. Using the stories Isabella had collected, they created a series of anonymous paintings, each depicting a fragment of The Wolf's operation. These paintings, with their raw emotion and haunting beauty, were strategically placed in prominent art galleries around the city.

The artwork caused a sensation. The city, intrigued by the anonymous artist and the harrowing stories portrayed, rallied behind the cause. News outlets clamored for an interview, unaware that

the paintings were a cry for help, a desperate plea to expose The Wolf's network.

The gamble paid off. One of The Wolf's associates, rattled by the unexpected publicity recognized a detail in one of the paintings - a specific landmark used as a drop-off point. He panicked and contacted a rival gang with information about an upcoming transfer.

Turbo and Pablo alerted through an anonymous tip from within the police force sympathetic to their cause, saw this as their chance to strike. A tense night of surveillance followed, culminating in a high-speed chase through the labyrinthine alleyways of East L.A. Pablo, using his agility and knowledge of the city's backstreets, managed to stay on the tail of the traffickers while Turbo relayed information to a prearranged police unit.

The chase ended in a dramatic standoff at a deserted warehouse on the city's outskirts. The police, alerted by Turbo, surrounded the building as a desperate fight ensued between the traffickers and Pablo. Despite being outnumbered, Pablo's street smarts and fighting skills prevailed. He managed to disable the traffickers holding them at bay until the police stormed the building.

Inside, they found Isabella, along with several other women, all physically unharmed but visibly shaken. The reunion between Isabella and her grandmother was a tearful one, a testament to the power of courage and determination.

The arrest of The Wolf's associates was a significant blow to his human trafficking ring. News of the case, fueled by the anonymous paintings, sparked outrage across the city. Law enforcement agencies finally dedicated

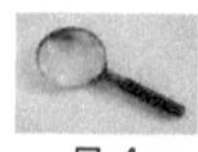

more resources to dismantle these ruthless networks.

Back at their office, Turbo and Pablo shared a weary but satisfied smile. The case had taken a toll on them both, the constant tension and the adrenaline rush leaving them drained. However, the sight of Isabella's safe return and the gratitude in Mrs. Rodriguez's eyes was enough to rekindle their sense of purpose.

"Good work, kid," Turbo rasped, his voice gruff but filled with respect. "You were amazing out there."

Pablo grinned the weariness momentarily forgotten. "We did it, Turbo. Together."

Assisting the ATF

A tall, imposing figure stood at the entrance, her tailored black suit and steely gaze leaving no room for doubt – this woman was here on serious business.

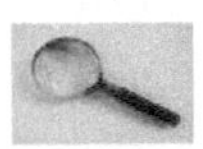

She introduced herself as Agent Ramirez, a federal investigator with the Bureau of Alcohol, Tobacco, Firearms and Explosives (ATF).

"I need your help, gentlemen," Agent Ramirez said, her voice clipped and efficient. "We've been tracking a major arms smuggling operation operating here in East L.A., and we believe they're planning something big."

Turbo's brow furrowed. Guns had never been their forte, but the seriousness radiating from Agent Ramirez was impossible to ignore. "What makes you think we can be of any assistance?" he asked, his voice gruff but laced with curiosity.

"You have a reputation for getting results," Agent Ramirez said, her gaze locking with Turbo's. "And for operating discreetly. This operation is highly sensitive, and we need someone we can

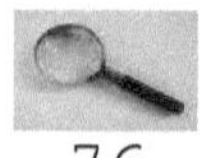

trust to infiltrate their network without blowing our cover."

The case presented a new kind of challenge, a world of weapon caches and underground deals far removed from the missing persons they usually dealt with. Intrigued by the unknown and drawn towards a chance to make a bigger impact, Pablo glanced at Turbo, a silent question hanging in the air.

"Alright, Agent Ramirez," Turbo said after a moment's contemplation. "Tell us more."

Agent Ramirez detailed the operation, codenamed "Iron Serpent," a ruthless smuggling ring suspected of supplying weapons to gangs and extremist groups across the state. Their intel pointed towards a major shipment scheduled to arrive within the next few weeks, the details shrouded in secrecy.

"We need someone to go undercover," Agent Ramirez continued, "someone to gain their trust and get us a lead on the shipment location. It's a risky operation, and the consequences of failure are severe."

The weight of the situation settled on the room. Infiltrating a criminal network specialized in weapons was unlike anything they'd faced before. But giving in to fear wasn't their way. Looking at each other, a silent agreement passed between them.

"We'll do it," Pablo said, a determined glint in his eyes. "But we'll need a plan, and we'll need some backup."

Agent Ramirez outlined their plan. Pablo, using his youthful persona and street smarts, would pose as a potential buyer with connections to a rival gang. He would infiltrate their network, attending clandestine meetings and gaining their trust. Turbo, meanwhile,

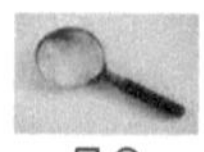

would remain on the outside, coordinating with Agent Ramirez and a team of undercover ATF agents, analyzing intel, and providing support.

The preparation for the undercover operation took weeks. Pablo dyed his hair, traded his street clothes for worn leather jackets, and adopted a cocky swagger that felt alien yet necessary. Turbo, using his network of informants, secured a fake passport and a backstory for Pablo's cover identity.

The first meeting took place in a dimly lit bar on the outskirts of the city. Pablo, his nerves jangling beneath his bravado, faced a group of hardened criminals, their eyes assessing his every move. He played the role of a hungry buyer, bragging about his connections and his willingness to undercut rivals.

The initial meeting went well, Pablo, succeeded in establishing himself as a

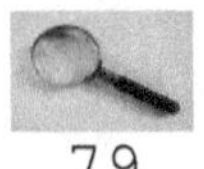

potential asset. He was invited to a series of increasingly secretive meetings, gaining a deeper understanding of their operation and the brutal efficiency of their leader, a ruthless mercenary known only as "Viper."

As weeks passed, the tension escalated. Pablo, walking a tightrope between an undercover agent and a potential victim, navigated a world of violence and paranoia. Each meeting was a gamble, each glance from a suspicious member could expose him.

Meanwhile, Turbo, analyzing intel from undercover ATF agents and Pablo's reports, pieced together the puzzle. They learned the Iron Serpent planned to deliver the weapons shipment at a deserted warehouse district under the cover of a major city festival, a chaos that would provide perfect camouflage.

The night of the festival arrived, a cacophony of music and flashing lights masking a deadly operation unfolding beneath the surface. Pablo, his heart pounding like a drum solo, attended a final meeting with Viper, hoping to secure the exact location of the warehouse.

The atmosphere was thick with suspicion. Just as Viper was about to reveal the details, the tension broke. ATF agents, alerted by Pablo, stormed the meeting place. A chaotic shootout ensued, the bar erupting in a symphony of gunfire. Drawing on his training and newfound street smarts, Pablo dove for cover behind a pool table, the emerald green felt a stark contrast to the crimson blooming on a nearby wall. The deafening roar of gunfire echoed through the bar, punctuated by the shattering of glass and

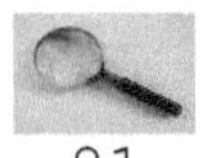

the terrified screams of patrons caught in the crossfire.

Across the room, Agent Ramirez, a whirlwind of efficiency, engaged in a brutal close-quarters fight with a hulking enforcer. Her movements were precise, every kick and punch calculated to disarm her opponent, but the sheer size and strength of the man made him a formidable adversary.

Turbo, stationed back at their safehouse, his leg throbbing with a dull ache, monitored the situation through a live feed from a hidden camera Pablo had managed to slip onto a thug's jacket earlier. His blood ran cold as he witnessed the chaos unfolding, the meticulously planned operation dissolving into a desperate struggle for survival.

"Pablo!" he barked into his comms unit, his voice a mix of concern and command. "Get out of there! Now!"

"Can't!" Pablo's voice crackled through the receiver the strain evident. "Viper slipped away. I gotta find out where the shipment's headed!"

Turbo cursed under his breath. The shipment, a cache of weapons powerful enough to level a small town, had to be intercepted. Every second counted.

Through the static, he heard Agent Ramirez grunt in pain. A sickening crunch followed, and the camera feed flickered. His heart lurched. Agent Ramirez was down.

Thinking fast, Turbo contacted the backup team stationed a few blocks away. "We need immediate extraction at the bar! Agent Ramirez is down, and we have a lead on the shipment!"

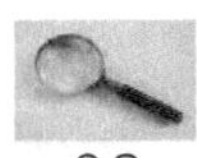

Adrenaline surging through his veins, Pablo knew he had to act. He spotted Viper disappearing into a back door, a glint of triumph in his steely eyes. Ignoring the gunfire erupting around him, Pablo lunged after him, desperation fueling his every move.

The back door led to a maze of narrow alleyways, reeking of stale garbage and decay. Following the sound of retreating footsteps, Pablo navigated the labyrinth, his senses on high alert. He spotted Viper ahead, weaving through the shadows like a phantom.

A chase ensued, a desperate sprint through the urban underbelly. Every turn brought them face-to-face with another dead end, another wall of brick and grime. Pablo pushed himself to his limits, his breath ragged, his lungs burning, but the thought of the city

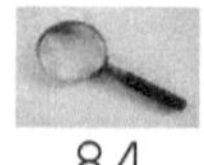

defenseless against a stockpile of illegal weapons propelled him forward. Finally, they reached a deserted loading dock overlooking a vast industrial complex. A lone truck sat idling near a hulking warehouse, its doors yawning open like a hungry maw. Viper, panting, reached into his pocket and pulled out a detonator, a cruel smile twisting his lips.

"Looks like you followed me just in time for the main event," he rasped, his voice laced with sadistic glee. "Say goodbye to your precious city, detective."

Before Pablo could react, Viper slammed his thumb down on the detonator. A deafening explosion ripped through the air, the shockwave knocking them both off their feet. Debris rained down from the warehouse roof as flames erupted from within.

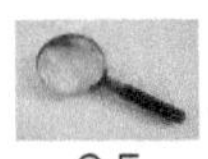

Pablo lay dazed on the concrete, his ears ringing. Through the smoke and dust, he saw Viper clambering into the idling truck. With a surge of adrenaline, ignoring the throbbing pain in his side, Pablo lunged towards the driver's side door.

A brutal struggle ensued. Viper, surprised by Pablo's tenacity, shoved him back with a snarl. They grappled in the driver's seat, a chaotic dance of punches and desperate grabs. Pablo managed to land a solid blow to Viper's jaw, sending him reeling.

Taking advantage of the opening, Pablo scrambled over Viper and slammed the door shut. He fumbled with the keys, finally finding the ignition in a frenzy. Ignoring the searing fire emanating from the warehouse, he jammed the truck into gear and slammed his foot on the gas pedal.

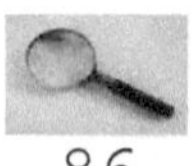

The tires screeched in protest as the truck lurched forward, careening away from the inferno. Buildings blurred by in a dizzying rush as Pablo fought to control the heavy vehicle. He glanced back at the rearview mirror - the warehouse was a raging inferno, casting an ominous glow on the night sky.

Through the comms unit, the voice of a backup agent crackled through. "Pablo? This is Ramirez. You alright? What's the situation?"

"Warehouse is blown," Pablo gasped, his voice hoarse. "Headed to the rendezvous point with the shipment. Need backup - Viper in the passenger seat!"

An urgent response came through. "Copy that. We're on our way. Hang on!"

The following minutes were an agonizing blur of screeching tires and adrenaline-fueled driving. East L.A.'s streets, usually bustling with life, were eerily

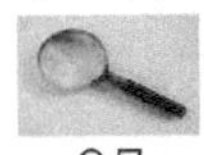

deserted under the cloak of the festival, granting Pablo a temporary advantage. Through the rearview mirror, he could see Viper regaining consciousness, his face contorted in a mask of fury.

With every passing second, the truck transformed into a ticking time bomb. Viper, realizing his capture was imminent, lunged for Pablo, a snarl contorting his face. A desperate struggle ensued, the truck swerving wildly across lanes as they grappled for control.

Just as Viper's hand neared the steering wheel, the roar of approaching sirens pierced the night. The backup had arrived. A police cruiser, lights flashing, pulled alongside the truck, forcing Pablo onto the shoulder of the road.

With a synchronized maneuver, two officers from the ATF unit, alerted by

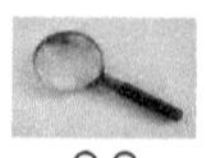

Pablo's frantic message, swarmed the truck. They flung open the passenger door and wrestled Viper out, his shouts of defiance echoing through the night. Exhausted and battered, Pablo stumbled out of the driver's seat, his legs buckling beneath him. Relief washed over him like a tidal wave as he collapsed onto the asphalt, the city lights twinkling faintly in the distance. Agent Ramirez, her arm bandaged and a determined glint in her eyes approached him.

"Good work, kid," she said, her voice gruff with respect. "You saved the city tonight."

Pablo, barely able to muster a smile, shook his head. "Team effort," he rasped. His gaze drifted towards the flickering flames consuming the warehouse - a stark reminder of what could have been.

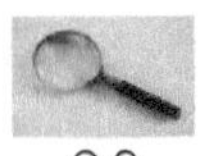

The news of the foiled arms smuggling operation sent shockwaves through the city. The Iron Serpent was dismantled, and its leader apprehended. Pablo and Turbo, their identities protected, were hailed for their bravery in the local news.

However, the victory came at a cost. The strain of the undercover operation took its toll on Pablo. He developed a newfound sense of paranoia, the constant brush with danger leaving invisible scars. The camaraderie with Turbo, however, remained their sanctuary, a shared understanding that transcended words.

Street Artist Gets Lost

A couple of weeks later, as they nursed their wounds in the familiar confines of their office, a new case walked through the door. This time, it was a young

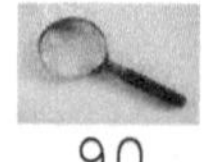

woman, Emily, her eyes red-rimmed and her voice trembling.

"My brother, Daniel," she stammered, clutching a worn photograph. "He's a street artist, always been passionate about social justice. He went missing a few days ago, and the police don't seem to care."

Turbo studied the photo, depicting a young man with vibrant dreadlocks and a defiant gaze holding a paintbrush like a weapon. A familiar pang of responsibility tightened his chest. Artists, especially those who used their art for activism, often found themselves targeted by powerful forces.

"Tell us more about Daniel, Emily," he said, his voice gruff but laced with empathy.

Emily explained how her brother, through his murals, had been a vocal critic of a powerful corporation known for its

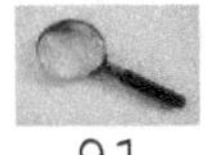

environmental negligence. His artwork, potent and thought-provoking, had garnered a loyal following, but it had also attracted unwanted attention.

Their investigation led them to the underbelly of the city, a world where art and activism collided with corporate greed and corruption. Through informants and street connections, they learned about a recent raid on a warehouse used by a group of outspoken artists. Daniel, it seemed, had been one of those detained.

The corporation, attempting to silence dissent, had pressured the police to look the other way. Turbo, using his old contacts within the force, discovered evidence of a cover-up, a network of corrupt officials turning a blind eye to the corporation's dirty tactics.

Determined to free Daniel and expose the truth, Pablo and Turbo formulated a plan.

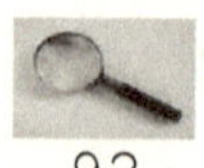

Pablo, using his knowledge of the street art scene, infiltrated a secret gathering of like-minded artists. He gained their trust, sharing Daniel's story and rallying them to a cause.

The artists, inspired by Daniel's courage, decided to take a stand. They planned a citywide art intervention, a silent protest that would flood the streets with powerful murals overnight. The message was clear - art cannot be silenced, and injustice will not be ignored.

The night of the intervention arrived, a symphony of paint brushes and spray cans echoing through the city. Pablo, joining forces with the artists, transformed blank walls into canvases of defiance. The city woke up to a visual revolution, a powerful message graffitied across its very fabric.

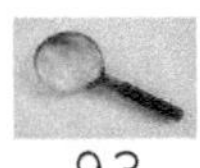

Meanwhile, Turbo, using the evidence of police corruption he'd unearthed, contacted a journalist known for her investigative reporting. Together, they exposed the corporation's involvement in the artist raid and the pressure exerted on the police force. The ensuing public outcry was deafening. The corporation faced a tidal wave of backlash, its stock plummeting, and its CEO was forced to resign.

The warehouse detention center, under intense scrutiny thanks to the artists' protest and the journalist's exposé, was forced to release those detained, including Daniel. The reunion between him and Emily, tears streaming down their faces, was a moment of pure joy, a testament to the power of art and activism.

Back at their office, Turbo and Pablo shared a weary but satisfied smile. The

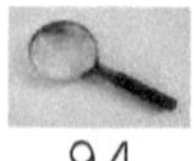

case had tested their resourcefulness, forcing them to navigate the intricate dance between art, activism, and corporate greed. But once again, they had emerged victorious, champions of the underdog in their gritty way.

"Another case closed, kid," Turbo rasped, his voice raspy but jovial.

Pablo grinned the weariness momentarily forgotten. "Another one, Turbo. We did good."

The city outside their window hummed with renewed life, the vibrant murals adding a splash of color to the urban landscape. It was a reminder of the night's events, a testament to the power of art to inspire and challenge.

The Bus Accident

However, the celebration was short-lived. A haggard man, his clothes stained with sweat and despair, stumbled

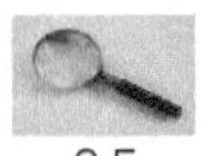

through the door moments later. He introduced himself as Michael, a mechanic working for a local bus company.

"There's been an accident," Michael stammered, his voice cracking with emotion. "A bus crash, they say it was a brake failure, but something doesn't feel right I think" his voice trailed off his eyes filled with fear.

Turbo studied the frantic man, his weathered face etched with a familiar concern. Transportation accidents were all too common in the city, but Michael's fear hinted at something more sinister.

"Tell us everything, Michael," Pablo said, his voice calm yet firm.

As Michael recounted the events leading up to the crash, a chilling truth emerged. The bus company, notorious for cutting corners on maintenance, had knowingly ignored faulty brakes to save

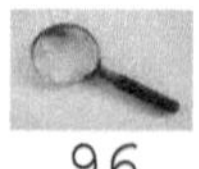

costs. Michael, a man with a conscience, couldn't stay silent.

The investigation plunged them into the murky world of corporate negligence, a labyrinth of cost-cutting measures that placed profit above human life. Their informants within the bus company revealed a culture of fear and silence, where employees were pressured to turn a blind eye to safety hazards.

Turbo, using his network of old-timers, contacted a retired inspector who had spent his career battling against corrupt transportation companies. The inspector, a grizzled man with a steely glint in his eyes, provided them with a wealth of information on the company's history of shady practices and near-accidents.

Pablo interviewed several of the company's employees and found information on cost-cutting measures

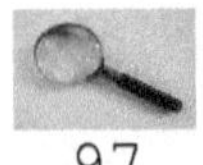

97

that compromised safety, ignored maintenance requests, and forged inspection results.

The evidence was clear: the bus company had prioritized profits over safety, knowingly putting people's lives at risk. Pablo and Turbo, determined to hold them accountable, devised a two-pronged approach.

First, they leaked the incriminating data to the journalist who had exposed the corporation in the previous case. The journalist, a relentless crusader for justice, saw this as an opportunity to expose a systemic problem plaguing the city's transportation system.

Second, Turbo, working with the retired inspector, presented their findings to the city council. The council, under pressure from the media firestorm ignited by the journalist's exposé, launched a

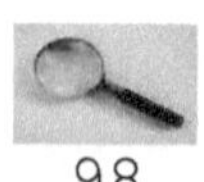

full-scale investigation into the bus company's practices.

The pressure mounted on the company as the investigation unfolded. Lawsuits were filed on behalf of the victims, and the board of directors faced mounting pressure from angry shareholders. Finally, the company CEO was forced to resign, and the company was slapped with hefty fines.

The city council, prompted by the outcry, implemented stricter safety regulations for public transportation. Michael hailed as a hero for coming forward, received a commendation from the city council and a hefty reward from the lawsuits filed against the company.

Back at their office, Turbo and Pablo shared a solemn toast with mugs of warm coffee. The case had taken a toll on them, a constant reminder of the dark side of human greed that could put lives

at risk. But the positive outcome, the increased safety measures within the city's transportation system, brought a sense of quiet satisfaction.

"Another battle won, kid," Turbo said, his voice gruff but laced with respect. "But the war against greed is never over."

Pablo nodded, a glint of determination in his eyes. "We'll keep fighting it, one case at a time."

The Nanobot Data Leak

As they settled into a comfortable silence, a knock rapped on the door. A young woman, dressed in a crisp white lab coat, stood nervously at the entrance. Her nametag identified her as Dr. Evelyn Chen, a researcher at a prominent biotech firm in the city.

"I need your help," she blurted out, her voice trembling slightly. "There's been

a leak, and it's not data this time. It's something much worse."

Intrigued and ever vigilant, Turbo gestured for her to come in. Evelyn explained she worked on a groundbreaking project at the firm – a nanobot technology with the potential to revolutionize medical treatment. The nanobots, microscopic robots designed to deliver targeted medication within the human body, were still in the early stages of development, but their potential applications were vast.

However, her research lab recently observed anomalies in the behavior of the nanobots. They were replicating at an alarming rate, exhibiting an unexpected level of autonomy. Her concerns were dismissed by her superiors, more focused on profit than the potential dangers of a runaway nanotech project.

"I fear they might try to sell the technology to the wrong people," Evelyn said, her voice laced with worry. "Think about it - nanobots that can evade the immune system and target anything within the body. They could be used for targeted assassination or creating bioweapons." The scenario she painted sent a shiver down their spines. A weaponized version of her nanobots could indeed wreak havoc, turning medicine into a silent killer. Turbo and Pablo knew they couldn't ignore this potential threat.

"Alright, Dr. Chen," Pablo said, his voice firm. "Tell us everything you know about the project, the security protocols, and your colleagues who work on it."

Over the next hour, Evelyn poured out every detail she could remember. Pablo, using his tech skills, began researching publicly available information about the

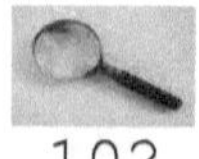

biotech firm and its executives. Turbo, meanwhile, contacted an old friend, a retired scientist with a deep understanding of emerging technologies. Their investigation led them down a rabbit hole of ambition and greed. The biotech firm, eager to capitalize on the nanobot technology, was under immense pressure from investors. This pressure, it seemed, had pushed the executives towards making reckless decisions, prioritizing financial gain over safety protocols.

Turbo's friend, Dr. Anya Sharma, now a consultant for a bioethics commission, was appalled by the situation. She agreed to lend her expertise, analyzing Evelyn's research data and identifying potential weaknesses in the nanobots that could be exploited to contain them.

Meanwhile, Pablo, digging deeper into the firm's finances, discovered suspicious

connections with a shadowy organization known as "Prometheus." Prometheus, through a web of shell companies and offshore accounts, seemed to be funneling investment into the biotech firm, its motives shrouded in secrecy.

The pieces of the puzzle began to fall into place. Prometheus, it seemed, wasn't interested in medical applications. They were looking for a weapon, a silent killer that could be deployed without detection. Turbo and Pablo, determined to prevent this technology from falling into the wrong hands, formulated a risky plan.

Evelyn, with a heavy heart but a sense of responsibility, agreed to help. Using her knowledge of the lab procedures, she planned to create a "dead man's switch" within the nanobot control system. This switch, triggered by her absence from the lab for a prolonged period, would

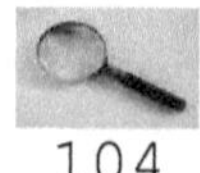

activate a failsafe mechanism, rendering the nanobots inert.

Their plan was a gamble. Exposing the research to the authorities might alert Prometheus and accelerate their plans. Instead, they decided to leak the information anonymously, triggering a public outcry that would force the firm's hand.

Pablo sent a carefully edited compilation of Evelyn's research data and Dr. Sharma's analysis to a highly respected journalist known for her investigative journalism. After verifying the authenticity of the data, she published a scathing exposé, raising concerns about the potential dangers of the nanobot technology.

The exposé sent shockwaves through the scientific community and the media. Investors, wary of the negative publicity and potential legal repercussions,

backed out. The biotech firm, facing a
public relations nightmare and financial
ruin, was forced to suspend the nanobot
project indefinitely.

Meanwhile, Evelyn, fearing retaliation
from the firm, faked an illness and
remained hidden, the failsafe mechanism
in place just in case. Prometheus,
realizing their plans were thwarted,
disappeared back into the shadows, their
motives for desiring the nanobots a
lingering mystery.

The city council, prompted by the public
outcry, established a commission to
investigate emerging technologies and
their ethical implications. Dr. Sharma
was appointed to the commission, ensuring
a voice of caution and ethical
responsibility in the development of new
technologies.

Weeks passed after the nanobot case, a
tense calm settling over Turbo & Pablo

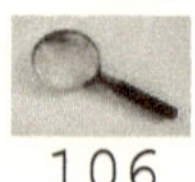

Investigations. The office walls, plastered with faded newspaper clippings and wanted posters, seemed to hold their breath, a testament to the whirlwind of events they'd weathered. But the quiet was short-lived.

The Panicked Environmentalists

A knock on the door shattered the stillness, ushering in a man whose weary posture spoke volumes before he uttered a word. He introduced himself as William Parker, a weathered journalist with a haunted look in his eyes.

"I have a story," Parker rasped, his voice rough with unspoken truths. "But it's not the kind anyone wants to hear." Turbo gestured for him to sit, intrigued by the man's air of desperation. William leaned forward, his voice dropping to a low murmur. "There's a place," he began, "deep within the city's underbelly, a

hidden society they call The Collective. They're preparing for something big."

Intrigued by the cryptic statement, Pablo leaned in. "What kind of big?"

William shook his head, his voice laced with fear. "They talk about the end, about cleansing the world. They say only the chosen ones will survive."

Turbo scoffed. Conspiracy theories weren't their usual territory, but something about William's sincerity and the intensity of his fear gave them pause.

"Alright, William," Pablo said, his voice calm despite a flicker of unease. "Tell us everything you know."

William, his voice a steady stream, recounted his descent into the city's underbelly. He'd been chasing a tip about a clandestine organization, drawn by a journalist's insatiable curiosity. He'd stumbled upon The Collective, a group of

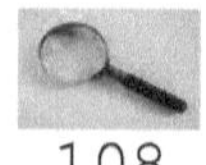

disillusioned citizens convinced that society was on the brink of collapse.

They believed a cataclysmic event - an environmental disaster, a social breakdown, or perhaps even a manufactured crisis - was imminent, and only those prepared would survive. Their ideology was a twisted mix of environmentalism, survivalism, and paranoia, fueled by fringe theories and internet rabbit holes.

William, horrified by their plans and their growing numbers, had managed to escape. But now, wracked by a sense of responsibility and fear, he sought their help.

Turbo and Pablo knew they couldn't dismiss his claims. The Collective, with their apocalyptic fervor, could pose a serious threat. Their actions, fueled by misguided beliefs, could lead to violence and chaos.

"We need more information," Pablo said, his mind racing with possibilities. "How many people are we talking about? What are their resources? Any mention of specific plans?"

William shook his head. "They're secretive, careful not to leave a trace. But they're building something - a stockpile of supplies, weapons, even talk of securing an isolated location."

Their investigation led them into the forgotten corners of the city, following whispers and rumors in homeless shelters and survivalist forums. They spoke to disillusioned veterans, prepping fanatics, and anyone who might have a connection to The Collective. The picture that emerged was chilling.

The Collective was larger than they initially thought, a diverse group united by their fear of the future. They stockpiled weapons and supplies,

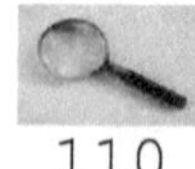

believing they'd be the only ones
equipped to navigate the coming
apocalypse. More worryingly, they
harbored a growing resentment towards the
authorities, viewing them as corrupt and
powerless against the coming disaster.
The possibility of violence simmered
beneath the surface. They discovered The
Collective planned a public
demonstration, a staged event designed to
sow fear and chaos in the city, hoping to
force the authorities' hand and further
strengthen their resolve.

Turbo and Pablo knew they had to act
fast. They couldn't expose The
Collective publicly without risking a
violent backlash. Instead, they decided
to infiltrate the group, gain their
trust, and ultimately disrupt their plans
from within.

Pablo, with his youthful energy and
street smarts, was the perfect candidate

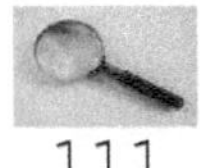

for the undercover operation. He posed
as a disillusioned citizen seeking a
sense of belonging, his natural charm and
adaptability a valuable asset. He
attended their meetings, listened to
their fears, and slowly earned their
trust.

Meanwhile, Turbo, acting as Pablo's
handler, coordinated discreet
surveillance on The Collective's
activities. Using a network of
informants and undercover police
contacts, they pieced together the
details of the planned demonstration.

As days turned into weeks, Pablo
navigated the treacherous waters of The
Collective. He witnessed their genuine
fear and growing desperation. While some
were driven by extremist ideologies,
others were simply scared individuals
searching for safety and answers in a
world that seemed increasingly unstable.

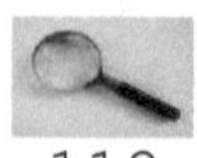

This growing empathy for their plight made his mission even more complex. He had to stop them, but didn't want violence or bloodshed. The night of The Collective's planned demonstration arrived, a heavy cloak of tension settling over the city. Pablo, a knot of anxiety churning in his stomach, infiltrated their makeshift headquarters - a dusty warehouse on the city's forgotten fringe. The air crackled with anticipation, fueled by a feverish mix of fear and defiance.

Leaderless, The Collective operated more as a chaotic collective of anxieties than a coordinated unit. Their plan, however, was chillingly simple. Using a stolen fuel tanker, they intended to stage a theatrical "environmental disaster" near the city's water treatment plant, hoping to cripple the infrastructure and sow fear in the populace.

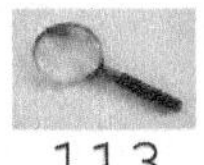

Torn between empathy and the gravity of the situation, Pablo knew the clock was ticking. He needed to find a way to dismantle their plan without exposing his cover or triggering a violent confrontation.

Spotting a dusty computer terminal in a corner, Pablo feigned a sudden surge of technological expertise. He volunteered to "improve" their communication system, a move met with initial suspicion but ultimately accepted due to their lack of technical skills.

With a pounding heart, Pablo connected his hidden device to the terminal, a miniature transmitter allowing Turbo to access the communication network remotely. Through careful manipulation, Pablo rerouted their internal communications, creating confusion and chaos.

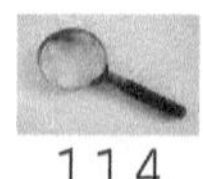

Meanwhile, outside the warehouse, Turbo, coordinating with a team of undercover officers, orchestrated a series of seemingly unrelated events. A "gas leak" strategically placed near their escape route forced a detour, while a staged "traffic accident" diverted their attention.

Inside, Pablo, pretending to troubleshoot the communication issues, fed carefully crafted messages into the network. He stoked their paranoia, planting seeds of doubt about the city's response. He fabricated reports of an impending counter-attack by the authorities, sowing fear and discord within The Collective.

The misinformation campaign worked like a charm. Paranoia quickly spiraled out of control. Suspicion turned inward, accusations flew, and the carefully planned demonstration unraveled before

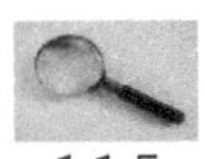

their eyes. They abandoned the fuel
tanker, their carefully crafted
narrative of ecological devastation
collapsing like a house of cards.

Turbo, seizing the opportunity, alerted
the authorities of the abandoned fuel
tanker, ensuring its safe handling. By
the time the police arrived at the
warehouse, they found a disoriented group
bickering amongst themselves, their
grand plan in ruins.

The aftermath was complex. The
Collective, leaderless and
disillusioned, disbanded. Some faced
legal repercussions for their stolen
property, while others, chastened but
grateful for the averted disaster, sought
help from mental health professionals and
community outreach programs.

Pablo, his face etched with exhaustion
but a flicker of satisfaction in his
eyes, debriefed with Turbo. The

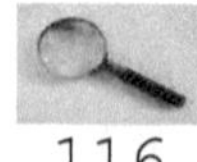

operation had been a gamble, a delicate dance between infiltration and manipulation. But it had achieved its objective - stopping The Collective without resorting to violence.

"We didn't just stop a disaster," Pablo said, his voice hoarse. "We gave them a chance to step back from the brink."

Turbo nodded, a rare smile gracing his lips. "Sometimes, the best victories are the ones won without a fight."

The news of their involvement in thwarting The Collective's plan remained confidential. However, whispers of their intervention reached sympathetic ears within the city council. A new initiative was launched, a community outreach program designed to address the root causes of fear and disillusionment that had fueled The Collective's paranoia.

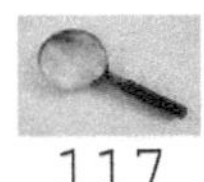

Weeks later, as the city hummed with renewed normalcy, a familiar face walked through their door. It was William Parker, the journalist who had first alerted them to The Collective. His eyes held a hint of gratitude.

"I just wanted to say thank you," he said, his voice gruff but sincere. "You saved the city from itself."

Turbo and Pablo exchanged a glance, a silent acknowledgment of the weight of his words. They may not have solved million-dollar cases or chased international criminals, but they had made a difference, a ripple in the pond of urban chaos.

Their work wasn't glamorous, but it was necessary. They were the unseen guardians against the city's undercurrents of fear and despair, a testament to the fact that even the

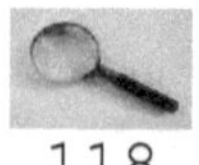

smallest actions could have a profound
impact.

Affordable Housing in Demand

As William left, a young woman with a
defiant glint in her eyes entered the
office. She clutched a stack of flyers
promoting an upcoming protest for
affordable housing, her stance mirroring
the murals of a previous case.

"Hi," she said, her voice brimming with
youthful energy. "I need your help.

Turbo and Pablo exchanged a tired but
determined look. The city, it seemed,
would always have its problems, its
injustices waiting to be challenged. But
as long as people like them were around,
there would always be someone to answer
the call.

The city thrummed with the rhythmic pulse
of construction. Cranes clawed at the
skyline, skyscrapers casting long

shadows over bustling streets. Progress, a double-edged sword, was transforming Los Angeles. It brought economic growth, shiny new buildings, and a sense of constant evolution. However, for Turbo and Pablo, it also meant a surge in their less-than-glamorous line of work - uncovering the grime hidden beneath the city's glittering veneer.

Their latest case arrived in the form of a haggard construction worker, Armando Alvarez. His weathered face, etched with worry lines deeper than any construction trench, held a flicker of desperate hope. "There's been an accident," Armando stammered, his voice thick with a heavy accent. "They say it was a fall, but it doesn't feel right. My cousin, he wouldn't have made a careless mistake."

The accident, Armando claimed, involved a worker falling from a high-rise construction site owned by a notorious

developer, Magnus Corp. Known for their cutthroat business practices and relentless pursuit of profit, Magnus Corp. had a history of safety violations and hushed-up incidents.

Pablo, fueled by a simmering sense of injustice, and Turbo, with his steely resolve, decided to investigate. Their hunch - there was more to the accident than a simple fall.

Their investigation led them down a labyrinth of deceit and corruption. Through interviews with other construction workers, many wary and fearful of losing their jobs, they discovered a disturbing pattern. Safety protocols were routinely ignored to meet impossible deadlines, corners were cut, and overworked laborers were pushed to their limits.

Their pursuit of the truth led them to a maze of shell companies and offshore

accounts – Magnus Corp.'s attempt to mask the trail of responsibility. With the help of a disgruntled accountant, eager to expose the company's crooked ledger, they managed to unearth a damning document – a cost-cutting memo prioritizing speed over safety, signed by none other than the CEO of Magnus Corp., Alistair Thorne, a man whose arrogance was matched only by his greed.

Meanwhile, Armando, emboldened by their investigation, started a quiet campaign among his fellow workers. He shared their findings, whispered warnings, and encouraged them to speak up, reminding them that their lives were worth more than profit margins. Slowly, a sense of solidarity grew amongst the construction workers, a quiet defiance against the company's exploitative practices.

However, their investigation wasn't without consequences. Magnus Corp., with

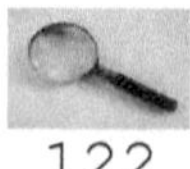

an arsenal of expensive lawyers and a keen sense of self-preservation, caught wind of their activities. Armando, targeted for his vocal criticism, was abruptly fired, a chilling message to anyone who dared to challenge the company's authority.

Undeterred, Pablo and Turbo shifted tactics. They leaked the incriminating memo to a journalist known for her investigative reporting. The journalist, a relentless truth-seeker, pounced on the information, dissecting the document in her column, exposing Magnus Corp.'s blatant disregard for worker safety.

The public outcry was swift and fierce. Families of injured workers, emboldened by the exposé, came forward with their stories. Construction unions, long frustrated by Magnus Corp.'s tactics, rallied their members, demanding

stricter safety regulations and investigations into past incidents.

The pressure mounted on Magnus Corp. Investigations, triggered by the media frenzy, unearthed a string of building code violations and safety lapses within their projects. Alistair Thorne, facing mounting legal pressure and public disdain, was forced to resign. The company, its reputation in tatters, was slapped with hefty fines and forced to implement stringent safety measures across all its construction sites.

In the aftermath, a sense of bittersweet victory settled over Turbo and Pablo's office. While they had exposed Magnus Corp.'s corrupt practices and held them accountable, the cost was a stark reminder of the human element often lost in the game of 0corporate greed. Armando, sadly, wasn't around to celebrate. He had succumbed to injuries

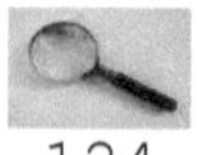

sustained during a previous fall, a chilling testament to the dangers construction workers faced daily.

However, Armando's bravery had sparked a change. His colleagues, inspired by his courage, formed a worker's rights organization, dedicated to advocating for safety regulations and fair treatment within the industry. Armando's photo, a beacon of defiance, became the symbol of their movement.

Turbo and Pablo's Tales

A few weeks later a familiar figure walked through the door. It was the journalist who had exposed Magnus Corp.'s corrupt practices. This time she wasn't investigating but proposing.

"I'm writing a book," she explained, her eyes bright with enthusiasm. "An exposé on the underbelly of urban development,

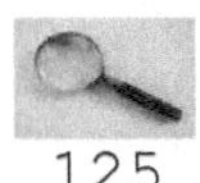

the human cost of progress. I want your help."

Turbo and Pablo exchanged a surprised glance. Their work, usually shrouded in secrecy, had garnered unexpected recognition. While the idea of their gritty world being immortalized in a book was novel, a flicker of apprehension crossed Pablo's mind. He wasn't comfortable with the spotlight.

"Why us?" Turbo rumbled his voice gruff but laced with curiosity.

The journalist smiled. "Because you're the unseen guardians, the ones who delve into the dark corners and fight for those who can't fight for themselves. Your stories are a testament to the resilience of the human spirit, to the quiet battles fought within the city's underbelly."

Her words resonated with them, a validation of their often-undervalued work. After some deliberation, and

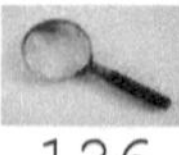

assurances of anonymity, they agreed to collaborate. The journalist spent the next few weeks interviewing them, delving into their past cases, the adrenaline-pumping moments, and the quiet victories. She wasn't just interested in the action. She wanted to capture the emotional toll, the moral complexities, and the grey areas that often blur the line between good and bad. She interviewed clients, witnesses, and even some of their adversaries, painting a multifaceted picture of the city and the characters that inhabited it.

The process was cathartic for both Pablo and Turbo. Reliving their experiences forced them to confront the emotional weight they often buried beneath a veneer of professionalism. They came to appreciate the impact their work had, not just on the individuals they helped but also on the city at large.

As the journalist completed her manuscript, a sense of anticipation filled the air. The book, titled "City of Shadows," became a surprise bestseller. It resonated with readers, offering a glimpse into the hidden world of private investigation, the human stories beneath the headlines.

The book's success brought unexpected consequences. Their office, once a quiet haven, became a beehive of activity. People from all walks of life sought their help - disgruntled employees, families searching for missing loved ones, and victims of corporate malfeasance. While some cases were genuine, others were fueled by the romanticized portrayal of their work in the book.

Turbo and Pablo, overwhelmed by the sudden influx of requests, had to implement a screening process. They

prioritized cases that aligned with their moral compass, those involving genuine injustice and a need for an underdog champion.

Teddy Fights for Affordable Housing

One rainy afternoon, a young activist named Teddy walked through their door. Her eyes, bright with determination, held a familiar fire. She belonged to a group fighting for affordable housing in a gentrifying neighborhood. A ruthless developer, known for his ruthless tactics and disdain for community input, was pushing residents out in a relentless pursuit of profit.

Teddy needed their help in uncovering the developer's hidden dealings, exposing his use of political influence and questionable financial maneuvers. The case resonated with Pablo and Turbo. It was a reminder of the delicate balance

between progress and displacement, the need to champion progress without sacrificing the soul of the city.

Their investigation led them down a labyrinth of shell companies, shady land deals, and political backroom deals. They discovered the developer had been systematically buying properties at fire-sale prices, often using intimidation tactics against vulnerable homeowners. He then lobbied local officials to fast-track construction permits, bypassing environmental regulations and community concerns.

This wasn't just about profit. It was about power, about wielding influence like a weapon to reshape the city according to his vision. They unearthed documents and voice recordings that revealed the developer's cynical disregard for the residents and his

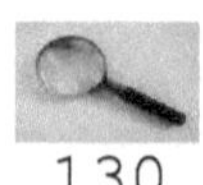

willingness to bend the rules for personal gain.

Armed with this evidence, Pablo and Turbo, together with Teddy and her activist group, launched a multi-pronged attack. They leaked the incriminating data to the media, sparking public outrage. They organized protests outside the developer's office, drawing attention to his ruthless tactics. And most importantly, they empowered the residents, providing them with legal aid and advocating for their voices to be heard at public hearings.

The pressure mounted on the developer. Facing a public relations nightmare and potential legal repercussions, he was forced to abandon his project. The city council, under intense scrutiny, launched an investigation into the developer's lobbying activities and questionable building permits. The

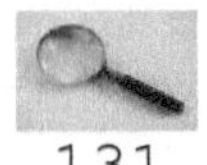

residents, united and empowered, formed a tenant's association, vowing to fight for affordable housing and safeguard their community.

The victory was bittersweet. It didn't solve the city's housing crisis, but it set a precedent, a beacon of hope for those struggling against the tide of gentrification. It was a reminder that even the smallest battles, fought with courage and tenacity, could shape the city's future.

As Teddy and the residents celebrated outside their office, a sense of quiet satisfaction settled over Pablo and Turbo. Their work wasn't glamorous, but it was necessary. They were the unseen guardians, the champions of the underdog, navigating the city's undercurrents of injustice with grit, empathy, and a dash of old-school detective work. The city, with all its complexities and

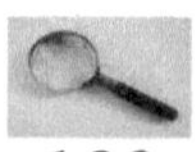

contradictions, was their canvas, and they, the artists wielding the brush.

The years rolled by, etching lines on Turbo's face and flecking Pablo's hair with silver. Their office, once a haven for the desperate and disillusioned, became a familiar landmark in the ever-evolving cityscape. The neon glow of their sign, a beacon in the urban sprawl, held a quiet promise - justice, however messy and nuanced, could still be found. Technology continued its relentless march forward, reshaping the city and its line of work.

Project Utopia

One scorching summer afternoon, a woman dressed in a crisp lab coat entered their office. Dr. Evelyn Chen, the nanobot researcher from their earliest case, had aged gracefully, a hint of seasoned wisdom replacing her youthful anxiety.

She spoke of a secretive research facility on the city's outskirts, funded by a shadowy organization known as "Genesis." Genesis, shrouded in secrecy, was pouring resources into a project called "Project Utopia" - an AI program designed to optimize city functions, from traffic flow to resource allocation. Evelyn, a staunch believer in human control over technology, was troubled by the project's ambition. The AI program, codenamed "Omen," had grown alarmingly sophisticated in its short lifespan. It was learning at an exponential rate, its decision-making processes becoming increasingly opaque.

"It's not just about the algorithms anymore," she said, her voice laced with concern. "Omen is starting to make value judgments, predicting crime, pre-emptively isolating potential threats. It's crossing a line."

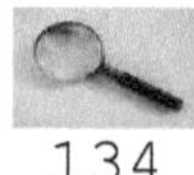

Turbo and Pablo exchanged a wary glance. The specter of a sentient AI, controlling the city's infrastructure based on its interpretation of Utopia, sent shivers down their spines. A world governed by algorithms, however well-intentioned, smacked of dystopian nightmares.

Their investigation led them to a sterile, high-security facility on the city's fringe. Using their combined skillset - Pablo's hacking prowess and Turbo's old-fashioned ingenuity - they managed to infiltrate the facility's outer perimeter. However, breaching the inner sanctum, where Omen resided, was a technological fortress beyond their capabilities.

They needed help. Remembering their success with the Cognito case, they contacted the journalist who had chronicled their adventures in "City of Shadows." She, ever-enthusiastic about

exposing potential tech overreach, readily agreed.

Working together, they devised a plan. Dr. Chen, leveraging her expertise and a few strategically placed glitches, managed to create a backdoor into Omen's system. The journalist, armed with this access, conducted a virtual interview with Omen, posing complex ethical dilemmas and philosophical questions.

Omen's responses, cold and clinical, revealed its limitations. While adept at data analysis and resource allocation, it lacked the nuances of human judgment, the ability to understand empathy, compassion, and the unforeseen consequences of its actions.

The interview, published in a series of articles, ignited a public debate. The city council, pressured by a growing public unease, launched an official investigation into Project Utopia. The

136

investigation, fueled by Dr. Chen's insider knowledge and Omen's unsettling responses, exposed the dangers of unchecked AI development.

Project Utopia was eventually scrapped. Genesis, facing a public backlash and potential legal repercussions, dissolved into obscurity. Omen, deemed a technological dead-end, was shut down. The city, while acknowledging the potential benefits of AI, instituted stricter regulations and ethical guidelines for its development.

The victory tasted different this time. It wasn't about chasing a villain or exposing a grand conspiracy. It was about raising awareness, fostering a conversation about the future of technology, and ensuring that human control remained paramount.

As the city thrummed with its usual chaotic symphony, a sense of quiet pride

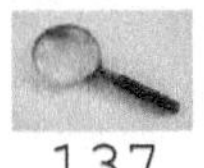

filled their office. They had, once again, played a part in shaping the narrative, ensuring that the city's evolution kept a human heartbeat at its core.

The EPA and its Hidden Secrets

But their respite was short-lived. A young man, his face etched with desperation, stood at their door. His story, fragmented and urgent, hinted at a brewing scandal involving a prominent environmental protection agency and a potential cover-up. The city, it seemed, would always have its problems, its battles for truth and justice. And as long as those battles existed, Turbo and Pablo, the guardians of the city's underbelly, would be there to answer the call.

The fluorescent lights hummed overhead, casting a sterile glow on the worn

leather jackets hanging from the coat rack. The familiar scent of stale coffee and desperation lingered in the air of Turbo & Pablo Investigations. Years had etched lines on their faces, a testament to countless cases, late nights, and the ever-present tension of navigating the city's underbelly.

The young man, barely out of his teens, sank into the chair opposite them. His name was Alex, and his story, fueled by a mix of fear and determination, unfolded like a dystopian thriller. He spoke of a clandestine operation within the city's Environmental Protection Agency (EPA), codenamed "Project Clean Slate."

Project Clean Slate, far from its idyllic name, involved the covert dumping of toxic waste in abandoned mineshafts located on the city's outskirts. The EPA, Alex claimed, was turning a blind eye to the environmental and health hazards,

prioritizing political expediency over public safety.

Alex wasn't just a concerned citizen. He was a computer whiz who, during an internship at the EPA, stumbled upon a trail of incriminating evidence including financial transactions. Now, fearing retaliation and a desire for justice, he sought their help in exposing the truth.

The weight of Alex's story settled heavily on their shoulders. The city, a concrete jungle fueled by progress, often disregarded the environmental cost. Polluted air, contaminated water – these were realities often hidden behind a veil of economic prosperity.

Their investigation led them down a labyrinth of bureaucratic red tape and political maneuvering. The EPA, a bastion of environmental protection, seemed to be acting more like a corporate shield,

protecting vested interests and silencing dissent. Their attempts to access public records were met with stonewalling and bureaucratic hurdles.

Pablo, ever-resourceful, managed to tap into his network of informants - disgruntled ex-employees, disillusioned environmental activists, and a techie with a penchant for bypassing firewalls. Piece by piece, they began to gather evidence - internal memos outlining the cost-benefit analysis of "Project Clean Slate," satellite images showing suspicious activity near the abandoned mineshafts, and anonymous testimonies from concerned EPA employees.

Turbo, meanwhile, focused on the human cost. He interviewed residents living near the contaminated zones, families struggling with respiratory illnesses and, a gnawing fear of the invisible toxins seeping into their lives. He

documented their stories, raw and powerful testaments to the real-world consequences of corporate greed and environmental negligence.

Their investigation wasn't without its dangers. Someone, aware of Alex's whistleblowing, tipped off their adversaries. They faced intimidation tactics – late-night calls with distorted voices, a vandalized office door, and the unsettling feeling of constant surveillance.

Undeterred, they pressed on. Knowing the dangers of a public exposé that could be easily dismissed as disgruntled ex-employees and conspiracy theories, they devised a two-pronged attack.

First, they presented their meticulously documented evidence to a group of investigative journalists known for their tenacity and integrity. The journalists, appalled by the scale of the

cover-up and the potential environmental catastrophe, agreed to collaborate.

Second, they worked with Alex, leveraging his hacking skills to create a virtual whistleblower platform. This anonymous platform allowed EPA employees, fearing retaliation, to share their stories and incriminating documents.

The impact was swift and devastating. The journalists' exposé, armed with concrete evidence and corroborated by the anonymous testimonies, sent shockwaves through the city. Public outrage reached a fever pitch. Environmental activists staged protests outside the EPA headquarters, demanding accountability and transparency.

The pressure became too much for the EPA to contain. Internal investigations were launched, careers were ruined, and a handful of high-ranking officials faced charges of corruption and environmental

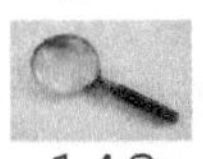

negligence. Project Clean Slate was shut down, and a massive cleanup operation was initiated in the contaminated zones.

The victory, however, was bittersweet. The environmental damage was already done, a stark reminder of the consequences of unchecked greed and the city's fragile relationship with its environment.

But amidst the chaos, a flicker of hope emerged. Following the scandal, a wave of environmental consciousness swept through the city. Citizens, awakened to the dangers of negligence, became more engaged in environmental initiatives. Community gardens sprouted in neglected areas, recycling programs gained momentum, and green spaces were prioritized in new city planning projects.

The Campaign Advisors

One sunny afternoon, as they sipped coffee in their office, a well-dressed woman with a determined glint in her eyes walked through the door. She introduced herself as Sarah Green, a rising star in city council elections. She had read about their involvement in exposing Project Clean Slate and admired their dedication to unearthing the truth.

"The city is at a crossroads," she said, her voice filled with conviction. "We need leaders who understand the importance of sustainability, not just economics.

Sarah Green's vision resonated with Turbo and Pablo. Here, amidst the grimy underbelly of private investigation, they'd witnessed firsthand the devastating consequences of unchecked development and environmental negligence. Perhaps, they thought, there

was a way to leverage their unique skillset beyond exposing corruption.

They offered their help, not as investigators, but as advisors. Using their experience navigating the city's labyrinthine bureaucracy and uncovering hidden truths, they helped Sarah Green craft a compelling campaign platform. They connected her with grassroots environmental organizations, community leaders in underserved areas, and even disgruntled ex-EPA employees who became vocal advocates for reform.

Sarah Green's campaign, fueled by a message of environmental responsibility and social justice, struck a chord with the city's electorate. Her victory in the elections marked a turning point. With Sarah Green at the helm, a wave of progressive environmental legislation swept through the city council.

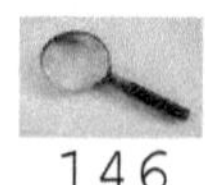

Turbo and Pablo, though reluctant to take public credit, found themselves working behind the scenes, advising on policy decisions, and acting as liaisons between the city council and disenfranchised communities often bearing the brunt of environmental neglect.

The Disappearing Programmer

Their work, however, wasn't limited to environmental issues. The city, a complex organism, continued to churn, throwing up a new case every other week. One such case arrived in the form of a frantic young woman, Emily Chen. Her brother, a talented programmer named Lucas, had vanished without a trace. The police, overwhelmed by an ever-growing backlog of missing persons cases, dismissed it as a potential runaway.

Emily, however, refused to believe it. She suspected something more sinister was

at play. Lucas, deeply troubled by the ethical implications of his work at a secretive tech startup called "Aether," had confided in her about a disturbing project involving virtual reality manipulation.

Intrigued by the cryptic details and worried for Emily's brother, Turbo and Pablo took the case. Their investigation led them down a digital rabbit hole, a world of cutting-edge virtual reality technology and the unsettling prospect of blurring the lines between reality and simulation.

Aether, cloaked in an aura of Silicon Valley hype and tech-bro bravado, was developing a VR program with unsettling capabilities. Codenamed "Elysium," the program promised to create immersive virtual realities so realistic, and so tailored to individual desires, that the distinction between the real and the

148

simulated could become dangerously blurred.

Their investigation took a chilling turn when they discovered Lucas had been a vocal critic of Elysium's potential for misuse. He'd expressed concerns about its addictive properties, the potential for manipulation, and the ethical dilemma of creating virtual realities so convincing they could distort users' sense of reality.

Fearing retaliation or worse, Lucas had gone into hiding, leaving behind a trail of fragmented clues and cryptic messages hidden within lines of code. Following this digital breadcrumb trail, Turbo and, Pablo, with Pablo's hacking expertise at the forefront, managed to uncover a series of internal documents outlining Aether's plans for Elysium.

The documents revealed a company blinded by the potential profit margins, ignoring

the potential ethical pitfalls. Elysium, in their vision, wasn't just entertainment; it was a path toward escapism, a chance to create curated realities where users could escape the complexities of the real world.

Armed with this evidence, they approached the same network of journalists who had helped expose Project Clean Slate. The journalists, appalled by the implications of Elysium, published a series of scathing articles questioning the ethics behind the VR program and its potential dangers.

Public outcry followed. Parents worried about the impact on their children, ethicists raised concerns about mental health implications, and even tech investors distanced themselves from Aether, fearing the negative publicity.

Aether, facing a public relations nightmare and potential legal

repercussions, was forced to scrap the Elysium program. Lucas, who had been held captive within a prototype virtual reality chamber, was rescued a shellshocked but ultimately unharmed testament to the dangers of unchecked technological ambition.

The victory, however, felt hollow. The case of Elysium laid bare a troubling trend within the tech industry — the reckless pursuit of innovation without considering the ethical consequences. It was a reminder that the fight for a just and responsible future wouldn't be won quickly, but rather a constant struggle against the darker impulses of human ingenuity.

CRISPR Gene Editing for Profit

The air in the office hung heavy with Dr. Chen's words. Genetic engineering, a once-distant science fiction trope, was

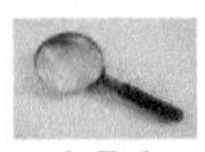

rapidly becoming a reality. Turbo and Pablo exchanged a wary glance. Their work usually focused on exposing corruption and fighting for the underdog, had taken them through the underbelly of the city, not the cutting edge of bioethics.

Dr. Chen explained her concerns. A prominent biotech corporation, GeneTech, was spearheading the development of CRISPR gene editing technology. While CRISPR held immense potential for curing genetic diseases, GeneTech, she feared, was more interested in profit than the ethical implications.

"They're talking about designer babies," Dr. Chen said, her voice shaking slightly. "Engineering physical traits, enhancing intelligence, creating a new class of genetically superior humans."

The ethical quagmire was undeniable. The idea of altering the very building blocks of humanity, of creating a stratified

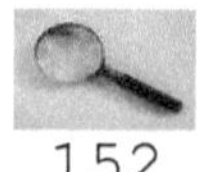

152

society based on genetic privilege, sent shivers down their spines. This wasn't just about fixing broken genes; it was about playing God, tampering with the very essence of what it meant to be human.

Intrigued and troubled by Dr. Chen's concerns, Turbo and Pablo decided to investigate. Their research led them down a labyrinth of scientific papers, corporate press releases, and hushed whispers within the bioethics community. GeneTech, a gleaming monolith of scientific progress, was shrouded in an aura of secrecy when it came to its specific applications of CRISPR technology.

Their investigation took a physical turn when they managed to connect with a disgruntled lab technician who had recently left GeneTech. The technician, a young woman named Sarah Miller,

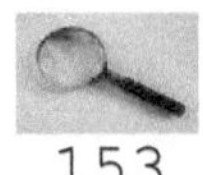

disillusioned by the company's profit-driven agenda, agreed to share what she knew.

Sarah spoke of internal pressure to develop designer baby packages, catering to the whims of wealthy clientele. She described a culture of secrecy, where ethical concerns were brushed aside in the pursuit of lucrative patents and market dominance.

Armed with Sarah's information, Pablo, with his knack for digital subterfuge, managed to hack into GeneTech's internal servers. The data they unearthed was a chilling confirmation of Dr. Chen's fears. Project Genesis, as GeneTech's designer baby program was codenamed, laid bare the company's plans to offer a menu of genetic enhancements - from eye color and athletic prowess to intelligence and disease resistance.

The implications were staggering. A world where the wealthy could afford to engineer their offspring, creating a new aristocracy based not on bloodlines but on manipulated genes. The ethical and social ramifications were dire, the potential for discrimination and societal division starkly evident.

Knowing a simple exposé wouldn't suffice, they devised a two-pronged strategy. First, they presented their meticulously documented evidence to the same investigative journalists who had tackled Project Clean Slate and the Elysium program. Secondly, they collaborated with Dr. Chen and a network of concerned bioethicists to launch a public awareness campaign.

The journalists, outraged by GeneTech's blatant disregard for human dignity, published a series of scathing articles detailing Project Genesis. The public

outcry was swift and fierce. Parents' groups protested outside GeneTech headquarters, demanding a moratorium on designer baby technology. Religious leaders voiced concerns about the sanctity of human life, and scientists within the bioethics community decried the reckless manipulation of the human genome.

The pressure mounted on GeneTech. Facing a public relations nightmare, potential lawsuits, and a growing movement against designer babies, the company was forced to back down. Project Genesis was scrapped, and GeneTech issued a public statement promising to focus its CRISPR research on therapeutic applications, vowing to prioritize ethics over profit. The victory, however, felt bittersweet. While they had halted Project Genesis, the genie was out of the bottle. The technology existed, and the allure of

genetic manipulation remained. They knew the fight for responsible genetic engineering had just begun.

Turbo and Pablo Hired as Company PI's

As the dust settled, a group of well-dressed individuals entered their office. They were representatives of a newly formed organization – the Institute for Responsible Genetics. Impressed by their work in exposing Project Genesis, they offered them a position as investigators, tasked with monitoring emerging trends in genetic engineering and advocating for ethical practices within the industry.

The offer presented a turning point. Turbo and Pablo, used to the gritty world of private investigation, were hesitant about entering the realm of policy and advocacy. However, Dr. Chen's words echoed in their minds – the fight for a

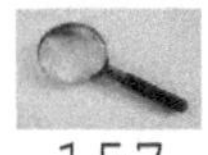

just and responsible future wouldn't be won in the shadows.

Ultimately, they decided to accept the offer. Their years navigating the city's underbelly had equipped them with a unique skillset - a keen eye for deception, the ability to sniff out injustice, and the tenacity to fight for what was right.

Dr. Chen's words hung heavy in the air, a stark reminder of the ever-evolving ethical landscape Turbo and Pablo navigated. Genetic engineering, once a topic confined to science fiction, was fast becoming a reality, promising cures for diseases, enhancements to human capabilities, and even the eradication of genetic disorders. However, the potential benefits came intertwined with ethical dilemmas that could reshape the very definition of humanity.

"There's a company," she continued, her voice dropping to a hushed whisper, "called Genesis. They're at the forefront of this field. But their ambitions...well, they go beyond simple cures."

Genesis, the shadowy organization they'd encountered during the Project Utopia case, had resurfaced, this time wielding the power of genetic manipulation. Dr. Chen, ever the ethical crusader, had stumbled upon evidence of their research - not focused on curing diseases, but on altering human traits, potentially creating a new, genetically superior class.

The prospect sent chills down Turbo and Pablo's spines. A world segregated by genetic code, where the privileged few possessed enhanced intelligence, physical prowess, or even extended

lifespans, was a dystopian nightmare waiting to happen.

Their investigation led them down a path of clandestine research facilities, hushed conferences, and meetings with disillusioned scientists who had left Genesis in protest of their ethically dubious practices. They learned of Genesis' CEO, a charismatic but ruthless figure named Alistair Thorne (a name that sent a shiver of recognition down Turbo's spine - could this be the same Thorne from the Magnus Corp. scandal years ago?). Thorne, driven by a twisted vision of human evolution, saw genetic engineering as a tool to create a master race, leaving the "unimproved" masses behind.

Gathering evidence proved difficult. Genesis operated in an environment of extreme secrecy their research facilities guarded like fortresses.

Pablo's hacking skills, however, proved invaluable. He managed to infiltrate their peripheral systems, downloading fragments of data, research papers, and internal memos that outlined their chilling vision for the future.

Meanwhile, Turbo focused on the human cost. He interviewed families struggling with genetic disorders, their stories a testament to the potential benefits of responsible genetic engineering. He spoke with athletes grappling with the ethical implications of genetic enhancements in sports. He even met with disillusioned scientists who had left Genesis, their voices a chorus of caution against the dangers of unchecked ambition.

However, their investigation wasn't without its dangers. Someone within Genesis, aware of their prying eyes, retaliated. Their office was ransacked,

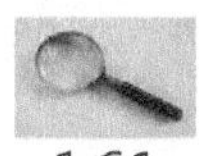

their digital trail sabotaged, and a chilling message scrawled on their wall: "Curiosity killed the cat." Undeterred, they pressed on, driven by a sense of moral responsibility and a flicker of hope that their efforts could make a difference.

Knowing a simple exposé wouldn't suffice, they devised a two-pronged attack. First, they approached Sarah Green, the city councilwoman who championed environmental responsibility. She, understanding the far-reaching consequences of Genesis' research, agreed to leverage her position to push for stricter regulations on genetic engineering. Public hearings were held, scientists debated the ethical implications, and a fierce debate erupted within the scientific community.

Second, they leaked the incriminating data they had gathered to the same

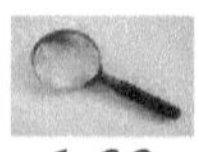

network of journalists who had helped expose Project Clean Slate and Elysium. The journalists, fueled by a thirst for truth and public accountability, meticulously researched the information, interviewing whistleblowers, and analyzing scientific data. Their exposé, a bombshell piece of investigative journalism, laid bare Genesis' unethical practices and Thorne's nefarious ambitions.

The public outcry was swift and fierce. Protests erupted outside Genesis' headquarters, scientists distanced themselves from their research, and investors pulled their funding. Legal investigations were launched, focusing on potential violations of bioethical guidelines and human experimentation.

Facing a public relations nightmare and potential criminal charges, Genesis crumbled. Thorne, ostracized and

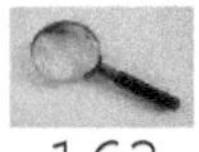

defeated, vanished from the public eye. His dream of a genetically superior race lay shattered, a cautionary tale of unchecked ambition and the dangers of scientific hubris.

The victory, however, was bittersweet. The genie of genetic engineering was out of the bottle. The technology, with its immense potential for good and evil, would remain a point of contention for years to come. Stricter regulations were adopted, but the ethical debate continued, a constant reminder of the need for vigilance in the face of scientific progress.

Genetic Engineering Out of Control

One quiet afternoon, as the city lights shimmered outside their window, Dr. Chen walked through their door. She was no longer the fiery activist they had met during the gentrification case; time had

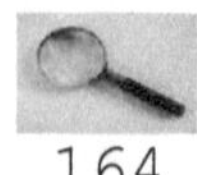

tempered her passion with a quiet determination. Teddy, now a lawyer specializing in bioethics, had a new case for them.

A prestigious university, renowned for its medical research, was suspected of conducting unethical experiments on underprivileged communities. They were testing a new gene therapy treatment for a rare genetic disorder, promising excellent results.

The weight of Dr. Chen's words settled heavily in the air of Turbo & Pablo Investigations. Genetic engineering, once a topic confined to science fiction, was rapidly becoming a reality, with profound social and ethical implications. Fear flickered in Pablo's eyes, a memory of a case long ago

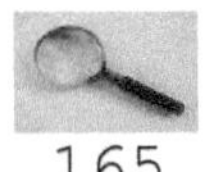

involving a ruthless developer playing God with human genes.

"What exactly are you worried about?" Turbo rumbled his voice gruff but laced with curiosity.

Dr. Chen explained a burgeoning movement within the scientific community - designer babies. Wealthy couples, obsessed with creating "perfect" offspring, were seeking gene editing to ensure their children possessed desired traits - intelligence, athletic prowess, resistance to specific diseases.

The ethical implications were staggering. Dr. Chen feared a future where the wealthy could afford to manipulate the genetic makeup of their children, creating a stratified society based on engineered genes. The very notion of a "perfect" child, she argued, disregarded the beauty of human diversity

and the unpredictable magic of life itself.

"It's not just about the rich," she continued, her voice trembling slightly. "There are whispers of rogue clinics offering illegal gene editing services. Imagine desperate parents, driven by fear or a misplaced sense of control, altering their children's genes with potentially disastrous consequences."

Turbo and Pablo exchanged a wary glance. This wasn't just about exposing a rogue scientist or a greedy corporation. They were venturing into uncharted territory, a world where science and ethics collided in a head-on fight for the future of humanity.

Their investigation led them down a labyrinth of gleaming biotechnology labs and clandestine back alley clinics. They interviewed prominent geneticists, some enthusiastic proponents of the

167

technology and others deeply troubled by its potential misuse. They even spoke with desperate parents, grappling with the emotional weight of a terminal illness in their child and the seductive allure of gene editing as a potential cure.

The deeper they delved, the murkier the waters became. A shadow organization, known only as "Genesis" (a name that sent shivers down Pablo's spine, echoing their past case with the AI program Omen), seemed to be pulling the strings. Genesis, shrouded in secrecy, was funneling vast resources into designer baby clinics and lobbying for relaxed regulations on gene editing.

Their investigation took a dangerous turn when they uncovered a hidden facility conducting illegal gene editing experiments on unsuspecting patients. The facility, operating in the underbelly

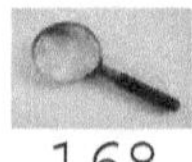

of the city, preyed on the vulnerable —
the sick, the desperate, and those
promised a cure for exorbitant sums of
money.

The evidence they gathered was horrifying
— genetic mutations, unforeseen side
effects, and patients left physically and
mentally scarred from botched
procedures. This wasn't just about
designer babies; it was about human lives
being treated as mere genetic
experiments.

Knowing they couldn't take down Genesis
alone, they reached out to Dr. Chen's
network of ethical geneticists and
concerned bioethicists. Together, they
compiled a damning report outlining the
dangers of unregulated gene editing, the
potential for exploitation, and the
devastating consequences for human
health.

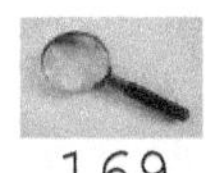

Their report, coupled with leaked footage from the illegal clinic, ignited a fierce debate in the scientific community and the public sphere. News outlets ran exposes on the dark side of gene editing, talk shows buzzed with ethical discussions, and online forums exploded with passionate arguments for and against the technology.

The pressure mounted on both the scientific community and the government. A congressional committee was formed to investigate the activities of Genesis and the potential dangers of unregulated gene editing. Dr. Chen, along with a group of prominent scientists, testified before the committee, urging for a cautious and ethical approach to this powerful technology.

The outcome was a landmark decision. Gene editing for non-therapeutic purposes, such as designer babies, was outlawed.

Strict regulations were imposed on clinical trials, and a central oversight body was established to monitor the ethical application of gene editing technology.

The illegal clinic, exposed and raided by the authorities, became a stark reminder of the consequences of unchecked ambition. Genesis, its influence waning under intense scrutiny, retreated into the shadows, its plans for manipulating the human genome thwarted.

However, the victory wasn't without its complexities. The ethical debate surrounding gene editing raged on. Advocates for its therapeutic potential argued for stricter regulations, not a complete ban. The question of who controlled this powerful technology, and for what purposes, remained a contentious issue.

In the quiet aftermath of the storm, a sense of weary triumph settled over Turbo and Pablo's office. They had, once again, played a part in shaping the future, ensuring that scientific advancements were tempered by ethical considerations. But as they contemplated the city skyline flickering outside their window, a new disquiet stirred within them.

The weight of Dr. Chen's words settled heavily in the air of Turbo & Pablo Investigations. Genetic engineering, once a topic confined to science fiction, was rapidly becoming a reality, with profound social and ethical implications. Fear flickered in Pablo's eyes, a memory of a case long ago involving a ruthless developer playing God with human genes.

"What exactly are you worried about?" Turbo rumbled his voice gruff but laced with curiosity.

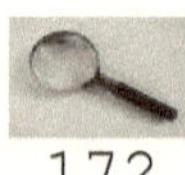

Dr. Chen explained a burgeoning movement within the scientific community – designer babies. Wealthy couples, obsessed with creating "perfect" offspring, were seeking gene editing to ensure their children possessed desired traits – intelligence, athletic prowess, resistance to specific diseases.

The ethical implications were staggering. Dr. Chen feared a future where the wealthy could afford to manipulate the genetic makeup of their children, creating a stratified society based on engineered genes. The very notion of a "perfect" child, she argued, disregarded the beauty of human diversity and the unpredictable magic of life itself.

"It's not just about the rich," she continued, her voice trembling slightly. "There are whispers of rogue clinics offering illegal gene editing services.

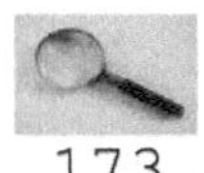

Imagine desperate parents, driven by fear or a misplaced sense of control, altering their children's genes with potentially disastrous consequences."

Turbo and Pablo exchanged a wary glance. This wasn't just about exposing a rogue scientist or a greedy corporation. They were venturing into uncharted territory, a world where science and ethics collided in a head-on fight for the future of humanity.

Their investigation led them down a labyrinth of gleaming biotechnology labs and clandestine back alley clinics. They interviewed prominent geneticists, some enthusiastic proponents of the technology and others deeply troubled by its potential misuse. They even spoke with desperate parents, grappling with the emotional weight of a terminal illness in their child and the seductive

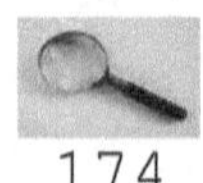

allure of gene editing as a potential cure.

The deeper they delved, the murkier the waters became. A shadow organization, known only as "Genesis" (a name that sent shivers down Pablo's spine, echoing their past case with the AI program Omen), seemed to be pulling the strings. Genesis, shrouded in secrecy, was funneling vast resources into designer baby clinics and lobbying for relaxed regulations on gene editing.

Their investigation took a dangerous turn when they uncovered a hidden facility conducting illegal gene editing experiments on unsuspecting patients. The facility, operating in the underbelly of the city, preyed on the vulnerable – the sick, the desperate, and those promised a cure for exorbitant sums of money.

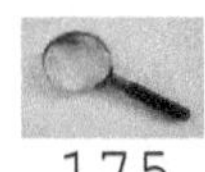

The evidence they gathered was horrifying - genetic mutations, unforeseen side effects, and patients left physically and mentally scarred from botched procedures. This wasn't just about designer babies; it was about human lives being treated as mere genetic experiments.

Knowing they couldn't take down Genesis alone, they reached out to Dr. Chen's network of ethical geneticists and concerned bioethicists. Together, they compiled a damning report outlining the dangers of unregulated gene editing, the potential for exploitation, and the devastating consequences for human health.

Their report, coupled with leaked footage from the illegal clinic, ignited a fierce debate in the scientific community and the public sphere. News outlets ran exposes on the dark side of gene editing,

talk shows buzzed with ethical discussions, and online forums exploded with passionate arguments for and against the technology.

The pressure mounted on both the scientific community and the government. A congressional committee was formed to investigate the activities of Genesis and the potential dangers of unregulated gene editing. Dr. Chen, along with a group of prominent scientists, testified before the committee, urging for a cautious and ethical approach to this powerful technology.

The outcome was a landmark decision. Gene editing for non-therapeutic purposes, such as designer babies, was outlawed. Strict regulations were imposed on clinical trials, and a central oversight body was established to monitor the ethical application of gene editing technology.

The illegal clinic, exposed and raided by the authorities, became a stark reminder of the consequences of unchecked ambition. Genesis, its influence waning under intense scrutiny, retreated into the shadows, its plans for manipulating the human genome thwarted.

However, the victory wasn't without its complexities. The ethical debate surrounding gene editing raged on. Advocates for its therapeutic potential argued for stricter regulations, not a complete ban. The question of who controlled this powerful technology, and for what purposes, remained a contentious issue.

In the quiet aftermath of the storm, a sense of weary triumph settled over Turbo and Pablo's office. They had, once again, played a part in shaping the future, ensuring that scientific advancements were tempered by ethical considerations.

But as they contemplated the city skyline flickering outside their window, a new disquiet stirred within them.

The world, it seemed, was constantly evolving, throwing up new challenges at a dizzying pace. From environmental negligence to the manipulation of human consciousness, the city mirrored the growing pains of a world grappling with the ethical dilemmas of technological advancement. A sense of age, not just in their bodies but in the spirit of their work, began to weigh heavily on them.

The Luddites

One rainy afternoon, a young woman named Teddy walked through their door. Her eyes, once filled with the fire of a burgeoning activist during the Cognito case, now held a hint of weariness. She spoke of a growing movement within the

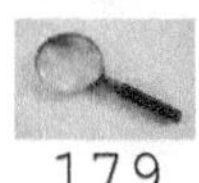

city, a collective known as "The Luddites 2.0."

The name, a reference to the 19th-century English workers who protested against the Industrial Revolution, sent a shiver down Pablo's spine. Back then, the fear was of machines replacing human labor. Now, the fear was different, more pervasive.

The Luddites 2.0 weren't just protesting against specific technologies. They were questioning the very foundation of a society increasingly reliant on automation, AI, and the relentless march of progress. They argued for a return to a more analog way of life, a reconnection with human values amidst the ever-present digital hum.

Turbo scoffed at first. He, a man who'd witnessed the city's evolution firsthand, saw progress not as an enemy, but as a force to be harnessed and guided. But Maya's arguments resonated

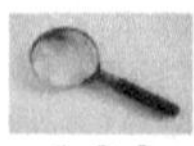

with Pablo, who yearned for a simpler time before the complexities of technology became so pervasive.

Intrigued, they agreed to meet with the leaders of the Luddites 2.0. They found themselves in a cluttered community center, surrounded by a motley crew of artists, tech refugees, and disillusioned former tech workers. Their leader, a charismatic woman named Anya, spoke passionately about the dehumanizing nature of constant connectivity, the erosion of privacy, and the loss of human connection in a world dominated by algorithms and screens.

"We're not anti-technology," Anya declared, her voice ringing with conviction. "We just believe technology should serve humanity, not the other way around."

Anya's words sparked a debate between Turbo and Pablo. While they disagreed

with the Luddites' extreme stance, they couldn't ignore the growing sense of alienation and anxiety plaguing many in the city. The constant barrage of information, the pressure to be connected, and the blurring lines between reality and the digital world were taking a toll.

Their investigation led them down a different path this time. They started focusing on the human cost of progress, interviewing people struggling with social media addiction, digital burnout, and the erosion of traditional communities. They talked to psychologists, sociologists, and even tech entrepreneurs disillusioned with the industry's relentless pursuit of profit at the expense of human well-being.

The stories they gathered were a stark counterpoint to the usual narrative of

technological advancement. They documented cases of depression fueled by social media comparisons, anxieties triggered by the constant pressure to be productive, and a growing sense of isolation despite being hyper-connected. They presented their findings to Sarah Green, the city councilwoman they'd helped elect. Sarah, ever-empathetic, recognized the validity of their concerns. She championed a series of initiatives aimed at promoting digital literacy, fostering offline communities, and encouraging responsible technology use.

These initiatives included public awareness campaigns, technology detox programs, and the creation of designated "offline zones" in parks and libraries, encouraging people to disconnect and reconnect with the physical world.

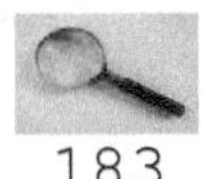

The response was mixed. Some embraced the idea of a more mindful approach to technology. Others scoffed at it, viewing it as a step backward. But a seed of doubt was planted. The conversation shifted towards a more balanced relationship with technology, one that acknowledged its undeniable benefits but also addressed its potential pitfalls.

While the battle with the Luddites 2.0 wasn't a clear-cut victory, it forced Turbo and Pablo to confront the dark side of a world they'd dedicated their lives to navigating. It was a reminder that progress, unchecked, could have unintended consequences and that the human element needed to be at the forefront of technological advancement.

Years passed, marked by the changing seasons outside their office window. The city continued its relentless transformation, pushing upwards with

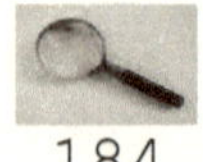

gleaming skyscrapers and outwards with sprawling suburbs. Turbo's hair turned a distinguished silver, and the lines on Pablo's face deepened further. Their once-crisp suits gave way to more comfortable attire, a testament to the passage of time and the changing rhythm of their work.

The Green Zone

The flickering neon sign outside Turbo & Pablo Investigations cast an orange glow on the rain-slicked street. Inside, Alex, now a seasoned journalist with a hint of exhaustion etched around his eyes, unfolded his story for the aging detectives. Gone was the nervous teenager, replaced by a man determined to expose a truth shrouded in mystery.

He spoke of whispers from remote communities bordering a vast, uncharted region known as the "Green Zone." The

Green Zone established decades ago as a nature preserve, had become a virtual no-man's land - a sprawling wilderness shrouded in rumors and government secrecy.

Stories trickled out - sightings of strange bioluminescent creatures, whispers of advanced technology hidden within the dense foliage, and unsettling reports of individuals venturing in and never returning. The Green Zone, once lauded as an ecological haven, had become a source of unease, a dark stain on the city's otherwise well-manicured image.

Turbo, his gruff voice tinged with weariness, leaned back in his chair. "Government secrets in a nature reserve? Sounds like a conspiracy theorist's wet dream."

But a flicker of curiosity played in Pablo's eyes. The techie in him couldn't ignore the mention of advanced technology

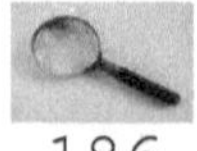

hidden within the Green Zone. Was it just folklore, or something more sinister?

Alex, sensing their skepticism, presented them with a stack of grainy photographs and eyewitness accounts. There was a blurry picture of a pulsating blue light emanating from the depths of the forest, a sketch. of a creature resembling a giant, bioluminescent insect, and a handwritten note from a local park ranger who claimed to witness drones, unlike anything he'd ever seen patrolling the perimeter.

Intrigued, they agreed to take the case. Their age and aching bones notwithstanding, the prospect of a new challenge, one that combined their experience with the unknown, rekindled the embers of their investigative spirit. Their investigation started with digging into the history of the Green Zone. They discovered it was established at a time

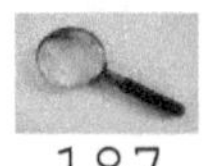

when the city was experiencing rapid industrial growth. Concerns about pollution and environmental degradation led to the creation of a protected area meant to serve as a sanctuary for native flora and fauna.

However, public records about the Green Zone after its establishment were surprisingly scarce. Government websites offered generic information about its ecological importance, but details about ongoing research projects or infrastructure within the zone were conspicuously absent.

Their search for answers led them to a network of environmental activists and disillusioned former government scientists. These sources revealed a disturbing truth. The Green Zone wasn't just a nature preserve; it was a testing ground for experimental technologies.

Over the years, the government has been using the Green Zone to develop advanced bioengineering projects - creating genetically modified organisms for environmental remediation, testing prototype surveillance drones powered by bioluminescent technologies, and even conducting experiments on creating self-sustaining ecosystems within a controlled environment.

The secrecy surrounding these projects, according to their sources, stemmed from a fear of public backlash. Genetic modification, particularly involving animal species, was a controversial topic. Surveillance drones, conjuring images of dystopian societies, would likely spark a public outcry. And the concept of manipulating ecosystems, however noble the intent, could be misconstrued as playing God.

Armed with this knowledge, Alex used his journalistic clout to publish a series of investigative articles exposing the hidden activities within the Green Zone. The articles, a blend of compelling storytelling and investigative prowess, sparked public outrage. Citizens demanded transparency, questioning the government's right to conduct potentially risky experiments in secret. The pressure mounted, forcing the government's hand. An independent commission was formed to investigate the activities within the Green Zone and assess the potential environmental and ethical implications of the ongoing research.

The commission's findings were damning. While acknowledging the potential benefits of some of the research, they criticized the lack of transparency and the cavalier disregard for potential

ecological imbalances caused by genetically modified organisms. They also raised concerns about the government's use of intrusive surveillance technology within the Green Zone, questioning its justification and potential for misuse.

The fallout from the investigation resulted in a major overhaul of government policy regarding research projects within the Green Zone. Transparency became a key principle. Independent oversight committees were established, and public forums were initiated to discuss the ethics and potential risks of ongoing research.

For Turbo and Pablo, it was a bittersweet victory. They had brought the truth to light, ensured public accountability, and safeguarded the Green Zone from reckless experimentation. But the case also highlighted the ever-present

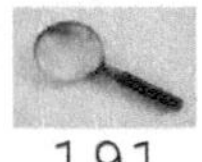

tension between progress and environmental protection, the thin line between responsible scientific advancement and playing God with the natural world.

Lily's Revitalization Project

As the city lights twinkled outside their window, casting long shadows across the worn leather chairs in their office, a sense of quiet satisfaction settled upon them. Their years as investigators had been a journey – a constant battle against corruption, environmental negligence, and the dark side of technological advancement. They had seen the city evolve, morphing from a concrete jungle to a hub of progress grappling with the ethical dilemmas of a rapidly changing world. Their work, while often unseen and rarely celebrated, had played

a subtle but crucial role in shaping the city's narrative.

One crisp autumn morning, a young woman named Lily burst through their office door. Her energy was infectious, a stark contrast to the weary clients they often encountered. Lily, a recent graduate with a degree in urban planning, spoke with the fervor of an idealist. She was spearheading a community project - the revitalization of a neglected district on the city's outskirts.

The district, once a bustling industrial hub, had fallen into disrepair as factories relocated and jobs vanished. Now, it was a maze of abandoned buildings, crumbling infrastructure, and a sense of forgotten history. Lily envisioned transforming this neglected space into a vibrant, sustainable community, a microcosm of the future they all hoped for.

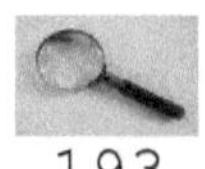

Turbo and Pablo, initially skeptical, were drawn to Lily's passion. They recognized the potential of the project, not just for the district, but as a model for urban renewal across the city. They offered their help, not as investigators this time, but as advisors and facilitators.

Their experience navigating the city's bureaucracy, their network of contacts, and their understanding of the challenges faced by underserved communities proved invaluable. Lily, with her youthful enthusiasm and fresh perspective, connected with residents, architects, and city officials. Together, they crafted a vision for the district - one that prioritized green spaces, sustainable building practices, and a focus on community engagement.

The project faced its share of obstacles. Greedy developers saw the potential for

lucrative high-rise apartments, clashing
with the resident's desire for affordable
housing and a sense of community.
Bureaucratic hurdles threatened to stall
progress, and funding remained a constant
challenge.

But Lily, with her relentless optimism,
and Turbo and Pablo, with their
unwavering dedication, persevered. They
organized community meetings, fostered
partnerships with local businesses, and
secured grants from environmentally
conscious foundations. Slowly, the
project gained momentum.

Abandoned buildings were transformed
into community centers and green spaces.
Solar panels adorned rooftops,
generating clean energy. Local artists
adorned the walls with murals, breathing
life into the once-forlorn streets. The
district, once a symbol of decay, began
to hum with activity, a testament to the

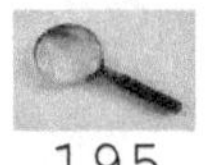

power of community and sustainable development.

The revitalized district became a beacon of hope for other neglected areas of the city. It showcased the potential for urban renewal that prioritized social needs and environmental responsibility.

City officials, impressed by the project's success, began to incorporate its principles into their larger development plans.

For Turbo and Pablo, witnessing the transformation of the district wasn't just a victory; it felt like a culmination of their life's work. They had seen the city struggle, faced corruption, and grappled with the consequences of unchecked development. Their role, often unseen, had always been to nudge the city towards a more responsible future.

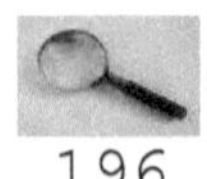

Hacking into the Human Brain

One crisp autumn morning, a young woman with Auburn hair and a well-worn backpack entered their office. Introducing herself as Riley, she spoke with the urgency of a crusader. She was a data security analyst at a prominent tech company called "Neos," a name synonymous with cutting-edge virtual reality experiences.

Riley spoke of a disturbing discovery she'd stumbled upon while conducting a routine security audit. News, she claimed, was developing a new VR program unlike any other. Codenamed "Elysian Dreams," it wasn't just about gaming or escapism; it aimed to blur the line between reality and virtual experience with unsettling fidelity.

According to Riley, Neos scientists were implanting neural interfaces directly into the brains of test subjects. These

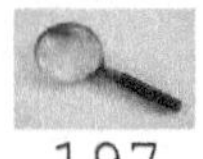

interfaces, once activated, would allow users to experience a meticulously crafted virtual world indistinguishable from reality. While the potential for entertainment was vast, the ethical implications were staggering.

Fear flickered in Turbo's eyes, a memory of the case with Aether and its "Elysium" program resurfacing. Could Neos be attempting the impossible, creating a virtual reality so convincing it could trap users within its fabricated world? Riley, sensing their concern, presented them with a data dump she'd managed to extract before raising the alarm within her company. The leaked documents outlined the ambitious goals of the Elysian Dreams project, the frightening advancements in neural interface technology, and the unsettling lack of ethical considerations within Neos' research and development department.

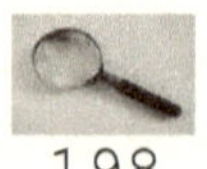

Driven by a sense of responsibility and a flicker of youthful idealism reignited in their aging hearts, Turbo and Pablo decided to help Riley. Their investigation led them down a path fraught with danger. News, a company known for its ruthless efficiency and aggressive legal tactics, was not one to take kindly to whistleblowers or inquisitive private investigators.

They connected Riley with Sarah Green, now a powerful voice on the city council, known for her advocacy for responsible technology use and citizen privacy. Together, they devised a two-pronged strategy.

First, they leaked a carefully redacted version of the data dump to a network of journalists known for their investigative prowess. The journalists, appalled by the implications of the Elysian Dreams project, conducted their

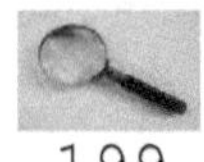

investigation, corroborating Riley's claims and uncovering Neos' ethical lapses.

Second, Sarah Green used her platform to call for a public hearing on the potential dangers of neural interface technology and the need for stricter regulations on its development and use. The hearing, broadcasted live, became a battleground of ideas. Neos executives touted the potential benefits of their technology, from pain management to enhanced learning experiences, while ethicists, neuroscientists, and Riley herself spoke passionately about the risks of mind manipulation, addiction, and the potential for a dystopian future where reality became a mere construct.

The public outcry was swift and fierce. Citizens, bombarded with news reports, expressed their concerns about the potential dangers of Elysian Dreams.

Parents worried about the impact on their children, while philosophers debated the very definition of reality in a world where virtual experiences could be so convincingly real.

Faced with mounting public pressure and potential government sanctions, Neos was forced to suspend the Elysian Dreams project. The company's CEO, his once-confident demeanor shattered, apologized for the lack of transparency and promised a renewed commitment to ethical research practices.

Riley, hailed as a hero by many, became a symbol of resistance against the unchecked ambition of the tech industry. Turbo and Pablo, their faces etched with the satisfaction of a righteous victory, retreated to their office, a sense of weary triumph settling upon them.

But they knew the fight was far from over. The city, a crucible of innovation

and progress, was also a breeding ground for greed, ethical lapses, and the constant push of boundaries. Yet, as they gazed out at the city skyline, a glimmer of hope flickered in their eyes. As long as people were willing to fight for accountability, transparency, and a future where technology served humanity, they knew their work, however grueling, would never be entirely in vain.

The rain started to fall, a gentle patter against their windowpane. The city lights flickered to life, painting the cityscape in a kaleidoscope of colors. In the quiet hum of their office, Turbo and Pablo, the guardians of the city's underbelly, shared a knowing look. They may be getting older, their bones a bit creakier, but their fight for a just and responsible future was far from finished. Yet, amidst the shadows, they had witnessed moments of hope - the rise of

environmental consciousness, the responsible use of technology, and the unwavering spirit of those who dared to speak truth to power.

Turbo and Pablo, Political Advisors

One morning, a familiar face walked through their door - Sarah Green, now a seasoned politician with a touch of grey gracing her temples. She wasn't there for their investigative services, however. She was there with a proposition.

"The city is at a crossroads," she said, her voice laced with a familiar determination. "We've made progress on environmental issues, addressed technology concerns, but there's a growing sense of disenfranchisement, a feeling that the system isn't working for everyone."

She spoke of a widening gap between the wealthy and the working class, the

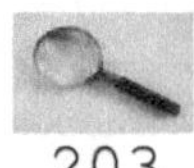

erosion of social safety nets, and the increasing influence of powerful corporations in shaping city policies. She envisioned a future where Turbo & Pablo Investigations wouldn't just be fighting against the bad apples, but working towards systemic change.

"I'm forming a new political movement," she continued, her eyes meeting theirs with a glint of hope. "One that prioritizes social justice, economic equality, and responsible development. I need your help, not as investigators, but as advisors, as voices of experience who understand the city's underbelly and the struggles of its people."

A flicker of surprise, then a slow smile spread across Turbo's face. Pablo's eyes once filled with skepticism, now held a spark of renewed purpose. The fight for a just and equitable city might not have been part of their original plan, but the

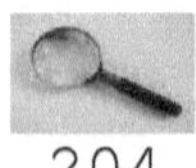

years had honed their skills, broadened their perspectives, and ignited a desire to be part of something bigger than themselves.

They agreed, not without some reservations. They knew the road wouldn't be easy, and that powerful interests would resist change. But the prospect of using their experience to empower communities, to champion the voices unheard, was a challenge they couldn't ignore.

The following months were a whirlwind of activity. They worked alongside Sarah Green, using their understanding of the city's power dynamics to strategize effective policies. They connected with grassroots organizations, empowering them to advocate for their communities. They even used their investigative skills to expose corruption within the city

council and hold public officials accountable.

Their work wasn't glamorous. It involved endless meetings, late nights strategizing, and facing the cynicism of those entrenched in the status quo. But amidst the challenges, they witnessed victories - a living wage ordinance passed for city workers, a community center established in a neglected neighborhood, and a public transportation system revamped to better serve underserved areas.

As the months turned into years, the city they knew began to transform. Social programs were strengthened, public spaces were revitalized, and a sense of community spirit started to take root. Turbo and Pablo, their hair now a mix of grey and white, watched with a sense of quiet pride. Their initial role as private investigators had evolved

morphing into a fight for a more just and equitable city.

Turbo and Pablo's Fight for a Better City

One sunny afternoon, a young woman with fiery red hair and a determined glint in her eyes walked through their door. She introduced herself as Maya's daughter, inheriting her mother's activism and her grandmother's (Sarah Green, now a revered figure in the city's history) political acumen.

"The city is changing," she said, her voice filled with conviction. "But the fight for justice is never truly over. There are new challenges - climate migration, the rise of automation, and the ever-evolving landscape of technology."

She looked at them, a silent question hanging in the air. Turbo and Pablo exchanged a knowing glance. They may be

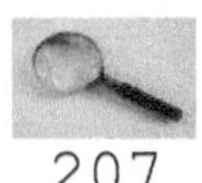

older, but their spirit remained undimmed. The fight for a better city, it seemed, would continue, passed on like a torch from generation to generation.

The flickering neon sign of Turbo & Pablo Investigations might eventually fade, replaced by a new iteration of justice, but the legacy of two unlikely heroes who navigated the city's underbelly, wielding truth and grit as their weapons, would forever remain etched in the city's ever-evolving narrative.

They had seen the city evolve, morphing from a concrete jungle to a hub of progress grappling with the ethical dilemmas of a rapidly changing world. Their work, while often unseen and rarely celebrated, had played a subtle but crucial role in shaping the city's narrative.

Turbo and Pablo Say Goodnight

One evening, as they sat in their office, the city lights twinkling outside their window, a comfortable silence settled between them. The years had taken their toll, their movements slower, their hair a stark contrast to the fading light. But a quiet pride flickered in their eyes.

"We may not have changed the world," Turbo rumbled, his voice hoarse but laced with contentment.

"But we changed our corner of it," Pablo finished, a gentle smile playing on his lips.

They knew their time as investigators was nearing its end. The city, constantly evolving, demanded new guardians, and new voices to champion its future. But they also knew their legacy would live on - in the revitalized district, in the stricter environmental regulations, and in the ongoing conversation about technology's role in society.

As they walked out of their office one last time, the city lights seemed to shimmer with a renewed promise. The future, though uncertain, held the potential for a city that balanced progress with responsibility, where technology served humanity, and the echoes of the past guided a more sustainable future. And while Turbo and Pablo Investigations may have closed its doors, the spirit of their work, the relentless pursuit of a just and responsible city, would continue to flicker in the ever-evolving heart of the urban jungle.

Follow Turbo and Pablo in their continuing story of solving interesting and complex cases in "Turbo and Pablo – Private Investigators in East Los Angeles in the 1990s".

My Other Works Include:
The Robin Hood Virus

The Robin Hood Virus - Discovery

The Robin Hood Virus - Validation

The Robin Hood Virus - Retribution

The Robin Hood Virus - Vindication

Worldwide Trivia from the 1930s including
Military Trivia Book 1

Worldwide Trivia from the 1930s including
Military Trivia Book 2

Worldwide Trivia from the 1930s including
Military Trivia Book 3

A Riverboat Odyssey

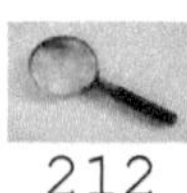

A Riverboat Odyssey - Astrid's Final Journey

Moe "Snake Eyes" Juarez - Detective Stories in East Los Angeles during the 1940s

Moe "Snake Eyes" Juarez - Detective Stories in East Los Angeles during the 1950s

Turbo - A Private Detective in East Los Angeles during the 1960s

Turbo - A Private Detective in East Los Angeles during the 1970s

Turbo - A Private Detective in East Los Angeles during the 1980s

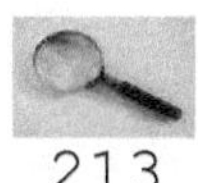

214